Flight to Gold

Donald J. Porter

PublishAmerica
Baltimore

First printing

ISBN: 1-4137-5169-5
PUBLISHED BY PUBLISHAMERICA, LLLP
www.publishamerica.com
Baltimore

Printed in the United States of America

1

THE FLIGHT

THE JAGGED, SAW-TOOTHED MOUNTAINTOPS protruded high above the valley floor, beautiful and ominous against a clear blue sky. A thick forest carpeted the countryside below, emphasizing the absence of any sign of human activity—no farms, villages, or roads.

The small, Piper Arrow aircraft flew a line close to the middle of the valley, the pilot taking great care to stay as far away as possible from the slopes on both sides. Charlie's precaution avoided the treacherous downdrafts next to the mountains.

The three passengers and pilot were flying from Centennial Airport near Denver to Montrose, Colorado, and baring trouble, the Piper Arrow would make the trip in less than two hours. Silently they gazed out the windows at the forbidding panorama of rugged wilderness below and cold, jagged rock above. The flight had to end eventually, and this foregone conclusion calmed their unspoken anxiety.

The pilot of the single-engine Piper calmly surveyed the horizon and gauged the rugged peaks.

"Good thing we don't have to cross that mountain range. Those peaks are too high." He shook his head, realizing such statements would only make his passengers more nervous, and made a mental note to keep his thoughts to himself.

Charlie's daughter, Sharon, shivered from the cold in the drafty cabin and said, "It's so desolate and deserted. No one lives in this part of Colorado, do they?"

Tom and Jean peered out the backseat windows at the lush forest below and the rocky spires that reached for the sky. "The scenery is beautiful, but it gives me the creeps. It's…it's massive," Jean said with purpose. "I can only say I'm glad we're up here, above it, I mean."

"Me, too." Tom laughed with an uncertain smile. "I could never have accompanied Lewis and Clark! No wilderness for me. I'll take city life anytime."

The sun bathed the airplane with streaks of gold as its rays slanted through the depressions among the spires. The glare flooding the plane hooded the landscape below in blue dusk.

Charlie turned his attention to the instruments, checking all the vital signs of the aircraft. His gaze stopped at the oil pressure gauge. It was a little below normal. *I'll have to keep an eye on that*, he reasoned.

"How much more time over this Godforsaken country, Charlie," Tom asked impatiently. It was a demand for reassurance.

"About an hour. Settle back and enjoy the scenery." Charlie drew a sharp breath as he glanced at the oil gauge again and realized the rate of pressure drop was becoming a real cause for alarm.

"Sharon, honey, I feel thirsty," Jean complained. "Could you pass me a bottle of Evian?"

"Okay. Hang in there." Sharon turned to pass the water to Jean, noting how tense she seemed to be, her face a wreath of worry. "We'll be back in civilization in no time." She smiled.

Charlie's eyes shot to the oil pressure readout again. "Damn it," he muttered, gritting his teeth as the needle trembled on red. The engine was losing oil fast. His brain immediately shifted to a new gear, the emergency gear wheel.

"Listen to me, all of you," he shouted over the engine noise. "It looks like we've got ourselves a real serious problem. We're losin' oil fast. Engine's goin' to quit soon." He glanced at Sharon. Her face was frozen with fear. She looked at him and choked back a cry.

"Listen," Charlie continued, "there's no field near enough for us to make an emergency landing, and I can't put down on those rocky mountain slopes. We'd break up for sure. But I think there is a way to get us down safely."

"For God sakes, how?" Jean asked. "It's solid trees down there."

"Damn it, Charlie. Didn't you think to check the oil before we left?" Tom shouted.

"Shut up, Tom, and listen. I'll have to set it down gently on the treetops. It can be done. I'll fly us down to just above the trees, level off, stall the aircraft, and pancake it down flat on the trees. We'll have a cushion of branches to settle on."

"Dad, can we survive a landing like that?"

"We'll be killed," Tom whimpered.

Jean sat, white faced, trembling, and silent.

"Tom, all of you, it's our only chance. The engine won't last much longer. I'm starting down now. I've picked out a place already. Sharon, look ahead at eleven o'clock. See that stand of trees that are lighter green than the other trees. Those are younger trees with smaller limbs. It'll be a softer cushion to land on no big branches or limbs to penetrate the fuselage. After we level off I'll cut the engine and turn off the electric switches. We'll stall out at about sixty-five miles an hour and come down with flaps and gear up. That way the tail will hit the trees first. When I yell, NOW, bend forward and put your arms in front of your face. Stay that way until the aircraft settles down. I'll put us in there as gently as possible. Tighten your seat belts."

"Oh God," Jean said weakly.

"We'll make it, Jean," Charlie assured her.

"Can I help you fly the plane, Dad?"

"No, not now, and don't even try the radio. Too many mountains for a signal to get out."

They were flying down parallel to the mountain range on their starboard side and close to its slopes. The monstrous peaks of rock rose menacingly above them. Even the rough slopes of boulders were now above them. Only trees were visible below. Dusk was approaching as the sun disappeared behind the mountains. Charlie would have just enough light to see his runway of trees. Luckily, the down draft of wind off the mountain slopes was minimal. He could control the airplane easily. It was time, time to level off. He pulled back on the control column and switched everything off.

Holding the nose of the plane up as long as possible, he intended to drag the tail in the upper branches to help slow down the forward motion. When the speedometer read sixty, he bellowed, "Now!"

CHARLIE

Charlie had flown many different types of aircraft. At fifty-five-years-old, he had over ten thousand flying hours. He had even flown some old vintage airplanes, including the B-25 bomber, the P-47 fighter, and the C-47 passenger plane in demonstrations and air shows. In recent years, his flying had been in many different types of single and twin-engine light aircraft. He was a big man, muscular and tanned, with piercing blue eyes and a firm, somewhat protruding, jaw. Gray hair and a few facial creases belied his youthful energy. Charlie walked with an almost indiscernible limp, the result of being careless when learning to fly. He had landed too long, plowed through a fence, and crashed into a deep ditch. His broken leg and its repair resulted in one leg being slightly shorter than the other. He should have aborted that landing, gone around, and approached the runway again. Charlie learned from that careless decision, and it was then he began to be a pilot's pilot. Double-checking everything on preflight inspections, he made safety a priority on all his flights.

Charlie's wife had died twelve years ago. He had loved her very much. Sharon was his only child, his treasure, the only treasure he needed or wanted. Though he doted on her, she had grown into a lovely, unspoiled woman who knew how to live properly and happily. She was the love of his life, but airplanes and flying came a close second.

Charlie Buckholtz was born to be a pilot. He learned everything about airplanes that was required of a professional pilot and could fly by-the-seat-of-his-pants, either by visual flight rules (VFR) or by instruments (IFR). His finely tuned hearing could detect the slightest engine problem. His eyesight was still as keen as it had been when he was twenty. Walking around his little Piper Cherokee Arrow, he made a last-minute check, looking at the ailerons, the rudder, the wings, the landing gear, everything. Charlie took great pride in his sleek little craft, always eager to slip the surly bonds of earth and dance in the skies above. His ritual walk-around inspection was always the same, ending at the tail. He paused there every time, looked down, and scuffed the ground with his short leg. Some would say it was a sign he was a superstitious man. Perhaps, but it had become automatic—a signal that all was well, and his bird was ready to fly.

On his way to the general aviation terminal, Charlie looked up toward the mountains. The weather looked good, no storm clouds were visible, and the atmosphere was clear. It was a warm summer day. After making a last minute check on the weather forecast, he would collect his three passengers and then take off for Montrose. He saw his favorite mechanic in the weather office. "Hi, Jake, is all my gear in the aircraft, including emergency supplies?"

"Way ahead of you, Charlie. It's all there strapped down in the backseat. I knew you only had three passengers this time."

"Thanks, Jake. You're the best mechanic in the universe. The plane looks in great shape and rarin' to go."

Charlie strolled into the passenger waiting area and gathered up his passengers. They went out on the ramp toward the waiting Arrow. Sharon thought her father was limping more than usual.

"Dad, are you all right," asked Sharon. "Is that gimpy leg acting up?"

"No, honey, it's just your imagination. I'm fine. We're all set to go folks. Climb aboard, and we'll soar into the wild blue yonder."

SHARON

Sharon glided down the stairs of their house as smoothly as if she were on level ground, as graceful as an autumn leaf blowing down the stairway, barely touching the edge of each step. Charlie looked up at her with love and admiration. She was a beautiful woman with regal posture, walking as proudly as a queen at her coronation. He had brought her up to be a lady.

Sharon's haughty demeanor melted as she hugged her beloved father. Charlie lifted her up to his level and kissed her cheek. She returned the caress with her one of her own.

"All ready to go to the airfield, my princess?" Charlie asked.

"Ready and eager, Dad. Can I fly the airplane today?"

"I'll think about your prowess as a pilot. Come on, let's get in the blue bomber and charge out to Centennial."

The blue bomber was Charlie's metallic blue 1959 MGA. When he bought the car it was about ready for the junk heap, and he had restored it to nearly mint condition. Cruising through traffic with the top down, Sharon's long blue-black hair streaming behind her attracted the attention of men and women alike. She and the car made a beautiful pair. But she remained aloof and was indifferent to the admiring glances.

Sharon was almost a replica of her mother. High cheekbones accented her oval face. Her chin jutted out slightly, not too much, a gene from her father. Her dark brown eyes could melt a suitor or freeze him, depending on her mood or whim.

"How many solo hours do you have now, Sharon?"

"Almost seventy-five, Dad."

"Tell you what. You can take off and climb to six thousand feet, and then I'll take over. Okay?"

"Sure! Wonderful! You'll see I'm a good pilot. With two years of flying you'll be proud of me."

"I better be proud because I'm also going to let you land the plane at Montrose. And I want to see you grease it onto the runway with minimum tire screech."

"Great, Dad, you'll see. I'll grease it in."

Sharon worked for an advertising agency designing layouts for women's fashionable clothing stores. She had learned her trade at the Traphagen School of Art while modeling part-time for local boutiques. Continuing to model, men offered more dates than she could possibly accept. Her father, long ago, had given her principles to live by concerning life and men: Don't even think of marriage until you're at least twenty-six years old. Experience life first, fall in, what you think might be, love a couple of times. Learn how to handle men and how to tell the good guys from the bad guys. Then get serious." Even though now she was twenty-six, Sharon had not begun to think of marriage. She was too busy with her job, modeling, and flying.

JEAN

In lower levels of Denver society Jean was known as "Miss Got Rocks." "Rocks" referred to the many impressive diamonds that adorned her fingers, wrists, and neck. Those in the middle ranks of the social order knew her as "The Witch." Of course, the "Got Rocks Witch" never heard these endearing names as she seldom left the confines of Denver's social elite.

Jean Prescott was born Henrietta Jeanne Proscino. She changed her name after attaining her first million dollars. Two deceased husbands left her several million more. And now, at forty-six years old, she was not married.

The title of witch assigned to Jean was accurate to some degree, but only in reference to her face. She was a dark complexioned woman of Italian ancestry with two facial features earning her that label. Her long aquiline nose had a small hump and her chin was a bit pointed. She resembled everyone's image of the Wicked Witch of the West. But that's where the chiding stopped because men were mesmerized by her magnificent body. Even now, no longer youthful, Jean had the figure of a Playboy centerfold, large, high breasts, a wasp-like waist, curvaceous hips, and long legs of insurable Betty Grable perfection. It was all the real Jean, no silicone, no liposuction, no tucks or lifts. Yes, it was body beautiful that made her a goddess of wickedly sensual, perfect womanhood.

Jean and Sharon had met at one of the boutiques that Sharon modeled for and an instant friendship had begun. Friends of the cloth to the end, silk, cotton, and rayon, Sharon enjoyed advising Jean on the latest fashions and helping her choose new outfits to add to her vast wardrobe.

"Jean, that pants suit would be perfect to wear on the fishing camp trip my dad and I are planning. We're going to fly our airplane to the nearest airport at Montrose next week. It's a fancy, full-service, beautiful place isolated in the mountains. You would love it. It's more than just a fishing camp."

"A fishing camp? Your airplane?"

"Yes, it's really Dad's plane a little single engine Piper Arrow. Nothing like your Saber Jet I've heard talk about. We fly low so you can see all the beautiful scenery."

Jean thought instantly: a new experience, a lark. Might be fun. "How long do you plan to stay there?"

"Four days. There's plenty to do if you don't like fishing, tennis, golf, and even bocci. Good music and dancing too."

Jean quickly trilled, "I'll do it. Sounds like a gay party. Would it be alright if I invite a friend to come along?"

"Yes, of course. We have room in the plane. There will be only the four of us. And Jean, just wear jeans on the plane. Save your pretty things for activities at the camp."

Jean thought about Tom. It would be the perfect little jaunt with Tom.

TOM

Tom Perdue, at thirty-six years of age, still hadn't found his way in life, mainly because he was lazy and had never focused on a career path. Successful, but unhappy, as a salesman in an upscale men's clothing store, he wanted the moon. For Tom that meant having enough money to do whatever he wanted. His plan to get what he wanted did not include ambition and hard work. It was to share someone else's wealth.

He was a modern version of Jekyl and Hyde. He could exude charm and pleasantness one day, and impatient, short-tempered egotism the next. Jean knew this about him, even though Tom was always a charming gentleman when he was with her. He was tall, handsome, and she enjoyed being with him. Knowing he yearned for the easy life of a gigolo, she knew how to use him. He was always a gentleman with her, and she could take him to any of the social functions in her strata of society. Also, he was most appealing and knowledgeable in sexual matters. He knew how to bring her to the pinnacle of desire and push her over the precipice of satiation. Tom had proposed to Jean, but she quietly and patiently rejected him saying, "Tom, you know I've been married twice before, and I'm just not ready to take the plunge again."

2

THE CRASH

THE ENGINE LASTED JUST LONG ENOUGH to position the aircraft for touchdown. The last rays of the sun were still illuminating the green runway. Gliding about a hundred feet over the treetops, Charlie aimed for the light green patch in the forest roof. Sinking slowly, speed down to sixty, nose up, tail dragging, Charlie eased the Arrow down to treetop level. The tail began brushing the flimsy light green tree branches, helping to slow it. Then the tail hit a larger branch, and Charlie had to fight to keep the nose up. "Stay down, folks. We're in the trees."

The nose of the plane began to sink. Charlie couldn't hold it up any longer. They were crashing through the treetops. The noise of branches scraping against the fuselage was fearsome. As they plowed through the small branches, the weight of the plane pressed them down into larger ones.

"Oh God!" Jean screamed as she covered her face.

Sweat dripped from Charlie's face. He wiped it with his sleeve. He tried again to lift the nose of the aircraft, but couldn't. Suddenly, there was a loud cracking noise as the right wing struck a thick branch. The wing folded up and back, and then tore completely off. Another branch shattered the side window Jean was crouched under. She screamed again as it penetrated the cabin above and behind her.

Charlie flung both arms up in front of his face as they careened on through the trees. Tom cried out as a branch broke through the window on his side and grazed his head. Shards of Plexiglas sprayed the cabin.

The airplane was settling down into the trees with forward speed down to about thirty miles per hour. Large branches crashed against the bottom of the fuselage but didn't break through. Another loud cracking noise told of the left wing buckling back against the fuselage. It effectively protected that side of the cabin.

"Oh Dad, when will this end," Sharon cried.

"Soon, honey, soon," he replied.

The windscreen in front of Charlie and Sharon disintegrated as they plowed into a large branch. Pieces of Plexiglas showered the four crouched people, but the branch broke off and didn't penetrate the cabin. Suddenly it was quiet. An eerie silence filled the cabin now that what remained of the aircraft had settled down into the trees. The cabin was canted slightly down toward the front and tilted somewhat to the right.

A low moan came from Tom as he straightened up. Charlie and Sharon sat upright at the same time and peered through the front of the broken airplane. Jean remained crouched down and ended her prayer, "Thank you, God."

"Tom, reach behind your seat, on the floor, and hand me the rope that is coiled there. Quickly," Charlie ordered.

"I'm hurt. My head got jabbed by a branch. Can't Jean reach it?" Blood flowed down the side of his face.

"No, Tom, you have to do it and right now."

Tom fumbled around and found the rope. He passed it to Charlie, groaning as he did so. He pulled a handkerchief from his pocket and pressed it to his gashed head.

"Is everyone okay? No major injuries? Only Tom's head?" Charlie asked.

Okay and dizzy were the answers.

"Sharon, see if you can open your door." The door gave way at the first push.

"I'm going to tie this end of the rope to the control column, then you uncoil it out the door 'til it touches the ground," Charlie advised. Continuing, he said, "It looks like we're about thirty feet from the ground. You go down the rope first, Sharon, hand over hand. Grip the rope tightly so you won't slide and get a rope burn. Jean will be next, then Tom. Quickly now, we've got to get out of here fast."

Tom asked, "Why so fast? Is there some other crisis? Haven't we had enough?"

Jean said with impatience, "Stop it, Tom. Charlie knows what we have to do. You don't."

"Sharon, look over the side to see if the rope is hanging free to the ground," Charlie asked.

"It looks straight down through the branchcs to me."

"Go!"

Sharon clambered out the door, grabbed the rope, and disappeared below the airplane. A minute later she shouted, "I'm on the ground. Come on, Jean."

Jean sat frozen in her seat, a look of terror on her face. She didn't move as she said, "I can't. I'll fall. Oh God."

Charlie reached back and shook her arm. "You can do it. You have to. We've got to get on the ground."

She came out of her terrified trance and climbed into the cockpit. On her way out the door her jeans tore on a jagged piece of doorframe. On down the rope, like a circus performer, she reached the ground.

"Come on, Tom," Charlie ordered. "When you get up front here, let me take a look at your head."

"Okay," Tom said weakly.

Charlie saw blood oozing from the gash on Tom's head.

"I'll bring the first aid kit when I come down. You'll be okay."

Tom climbed out, grabbed the rope, and was gone.

Charlie climbed into the back, reached into the rear seat, and retrieved the emergency supplies that Jake had put there. He pulled up the rope, tied it to the emergency box, and lowered it down. Then he grasped the rope and quickly descended to the ground. "Come with me, everyone," Charlie said firmly. "Over here to this little clearing. We need to take stock of our situation."

THE DEEP WOODS

They sat on old fallen tree trunks surrounded by huge pine trees. Jean was tending to Tom's wound. She took a bottle of peroxide from the first aid kit.

"This will sting a little, Tom, but I have to clean the cut."

"Okay, Jean. Go easy."

Forty feet away, the remains of the airplane rested precariously in the trees. It looked like a prehistoric mantis looking down on them. Suddenly there was a loud cracking noise as a branch broke. The Arrow settled further down into its bed of branches.

Gazing up at the trees about one hundred feet in front of the airplane, Charlie pointed as he said, "Look up there. We stopped just short of the bigger tougher trees. We were lucky."

"No, Dad. It was your skill as a pilot and your knowledge of the mountains that saved our lives. Thanks."

Jean immediately chimed in, "Thank you, Charlie, for getting us down safely."

After a brief silence, Jean said sharply, "Tom, don't you have something to say?"

"Yes," Tom said sourly without looking up. "As Hardy would say, 'this is a fine mess you've gotten us into'." He continued to stare at the ground.

Charlie sat there quietly. Jean got up and faced Tom saying, "Tom, let me tell you a little story I hope will teach you something. I have a son who lives in San Francisco. He is married and has a son, my grandson. His wife is a brilliant woman in many respects, but she has a glaring character flaw. She doesn't believe it is necessary to always say thank you when given something.

She justified this to me by saying her family was not in the habit of expressing that sentiment. Another time, her justification was that people should know of her appreciation even if she doesn't say thank you. To me, those are sorry pieces of justification. Everyone should know you have to say thank you when someone does something for you. Tom, Charlie just saved your life. What do you have to say?"

Pausing for thought, Tom looked up at Jean, then turned to Charlie and reluctantly allowed a weak, "Thank you." Maybe he was learning.

"I appreciate your thanks," Charlie said sincerely. "Now for the business of survival here in the deep woods. Sharon, you and I are going four or five hundred yards behind the aircraft to see if we can find the right wing. I want to see if it's visible from the air, visible to search planes. It'll be hard to find us. There isn't an Emergency Location Transmitter on the plane. I couldn't afford to install one.

Jean and Tom, you stay here. We won't be long. Oh, by the way, Tom, for your information, you have to get out of an airplane fast in crashes because of the danger of fire, fuel being ignited. Speaking of fire, Tom and Jean, gather up some branches and start a little fire here in the clearing. It'll be cool tonight. Do you have any matches?"

"A cigarette lighter," Jean said quickly.

"That'll work. Come on, Sharon. Let's go find that wing."

They followed the trail of broken tree branches behind the Arrow, bushes and underbrush fairly thick, but they were able to push their way through in a fairly straight line.

They came upon the wing about four hundred yards from where the plane had settled. It had slipped down through the trees and rested on the ground. Noting with dismay that the wing could not be seen from the air, Charlie and Sharon quickly returned to Jean and Tom.

Again, there was the sound of cracking branches as the airplane settled even further down into the trees. Charlie looked up at the space above the Arrow. The foliage of unbroken branches on either side of the airplane was hiding the Arrow from being sighted by search planes.

Tom was tending a small fire, putting twigs on it. They had done it right, clearing the ground first and making a small, warming fire.

Charlie rasped, "Where is the water jug? After a swallow or two, I'm going back up to the plane to get our luggage. I imagine all of you want some of your things. I can get to the luggage compartment through a panel behind the rear seats. Maybe there are a couple of blankets up there too. I suggest you start looking for small branches, leaves, moss, whatever you can find to use for cushioning a place to sleep by the fire tonight."

After a quick drink of water, Charlie started up the rope, hand over hand, and maneuvered his way into the cabin of the plane. As he got toward the tail, his weight caused it to sink a few inches further down into the trees. Removing the panel from behind the seats with a screwdriver from the emergency kit, he retrieved the suitcases and other luggage from the storage compartment and sent them down on the rope to the three waiting on the ground. Before he left the plane, Charlie took his thirty-eight revolver from under the instrument panel and slipped it into a pocket of his flying suit.

"Sorry, there aren't any blankets up there in the plane. You'll have to make yourselves as warm as possible with your clothes. Please don't drink too much of our water. We'll have to ration it. Get some rest as best you can tonight, and we'll talk about what's in store for us in the morning."

THE WATERFALL

The sun pierced the deep valley with strobes of golden light between the mountain peaks. Awake early, they were happy to leave their uncomfortable beds of pine boughs and leaves. Sitting up to drink instant coffee and eat four saltine crackers apiece seemed to ease their aching bodies.

"Dad, as we were approaching our tree runway yesterday, I saw a faint mist above the trees in front of us. Did you see it?"

"Yes, I did, Sharon, and I've been thinking about it. What could cause a mist or spray like that? The only thing I can think of is a waterfall. And that would be good news for us. Water is the most necessary requirement for our survival."

"But, Charlie," Jean interjected. "How far away do you think it is?"

"I would estimate about two miles from here," Charlie answered.

Tom groaned. "I can see it now. We slog through this forest, clawing through the trees and bushes to, maybe find a waterfall. Right?"

"Tom, if you would prefer, you can stay here while we find some water to drink," Charlie said patiently.

"Yes, Tom," Jean added. "Stay here if you like and hope the search planes see you."

"All right, all right," Tom blustered. "Sorry, I'm just not cut out to be a frontiersman."

A loud noise, almost like a gunshot, made them all flinch and look up at the remains of the Arrow. It had dropped even farther into the trees, breaking branches as it fell. Charlie sighed. "Even more difficult to be seen from the air now. Let me give you a picture of our situation. Normally, survivors of a crash should stay at the crash site and wait for search parties to find them. In our case, I think the circumstances call for different action. The airplane has settled so far into the trees that it's next to impossible for search planes to see it. The aircraft radio is useless, so we can't communicate. We'll have to live off the land because there are only a few snacks left. Some of the nuts and berries we find will be okay, but you'll have to let me check them to make sure they're not poisonous. We should be able to find some edible roots too. I have a little revolver and may be able to get us a rabbit or some other small game. And we might catch a fish or two if we find the river.

"Now, as to our location and the possibility of walking out of here to civilization. According to LORAN, we're more than halfway from Denver to Montrose. I'm pretty sure we're somewhere in the Gunnison National Forest. Not knowing exactly where, it's possible we have a thirty mile hike ahead of us."

"Charlie," Jean queried, "how long will it take to get out of this forest?"

"Maybe a week or ten days. It'll be slow going, and hopefully, we won't have to climb any mountains."

"How do you know which direction to go?" Tom asked.

"I've got that figured out. We were on course when we crashed. A few miles before the crash I spotted what I'm sure is Ohio peak. Its elevation is about twelve thousand feet. If we travel southwest from here we should come to Route 92 and perhaps the town of Maher.

Gather around me so I can show you on my navigation map. I've already marked where I think we are: this X on the red flight line. Here's Ohio peak. See here, we'll cross Route 92 near Maher on a heading of 230 degrees. I figure it's about thirty miles to Maher."

"Dad, we're sure lucky to have you as our navigator," Sharon said proudly.

"Come on, let's head for our water supply. Sharon, you carry the first aid kit. I'll take our emergency supplies. Tom, make sure the fire is completely out. Leave your party clothes here. We can't be burdened with unnecessary stuff. I've got a compass, so we won't walk in circles. Let's go."

Charlie led the way, heading just to the left of the airplane nose. He tried to pick unhindered pathways through the forest, while the other three followed in single file. After about a mile of trudging along, Jean pleaded for a break.

"Just a little rest, Charlie."

"Of course, Jean. We don't have to hurry. How are you doing, Tom?"

"Okay, I'll make it. Jean, would you check my bandage."

"Sharon, I'm glad you and Jean aren't wearing high heels. You're both dressed quite well for this trek," Charlie said.

After passing the water jug around, they started off again. Charlie put his hand over the pocket in which he had his pistol. He wondered what wild animals they might encounter. Bears and mountain lions surely lived in this area. Charlie and his companions were invading this pristine, uncivilized part of the Rocky Mountains home to all manner of animals. They plodded on, getting minor scratches from bushes and low hanging tree limbs. Suddenly Charlie stopped.

"Come here everyone. Look straight ahead."

Tom was the first to see it and said, "It's a river or a large creek. You were right, Charlie. It's our water supply. But where's the waterfall? Let's go get a closer look. Maybe we'll see something more down there."

They walked slowly down the slope through the trees to the river. Looking both downstream and upstream they could see only more river and tall trees. Charlie took the water jug from Sharon and filled it from a small pool between rocks. The water was cold and clear.

Jean joined Sharon as she bent down at riverbank and splashed water on her face. They sat on a log and looked around while Tom wandered downstream into some thick bushes.

Charlie called to them. "Come on. We'll go upstream toward the mountains. If there is a waterfall, we should find it there. Gather your things and follow me. I'd like to see the source of the mist we saw."

They plodded along the riverbank, going back into the woods occasionally when thick bushes or huge boulders barred their path. After walking only a quarter mile they began to hear the splash of a waterfall. The sound of rushing water falling against rocks and into a pool was unmistakable. Soon, coming out of the thick bushes and trees, they were able to see the splendor of the cascading water.

It was a beautiful sight, the water dropping fifty feet off the edge of a cliff to a rock ledge, then spraying another ten feet into a sparkling collection that resembled an oblong swimming pool. Though the falls were impressive, the river itself was narrow, hidden from view above by the lofty pine trees and branches, heavy with foliage.

"What a beautiful, idyllic place. It's my idea of the Garden of Eden," Sharon said.

Tom countered, "But where is the apple tree? Oh well, at least there's probably a snake nearby."

"Tom, you're too much of a cynic, not to mention pessimist," Jean chided. "This is so peaceful and lovely. I should buy a few acres here and build a camp."

Charlie, practical as ever, said in his commanding way, "All right, dreamers, enough. We'd better look for a place to stay tonight. Maybe we'll find a cave along the rock wall. It would be nice to get out of the rain, when and if it comes. Tom, you and Jean look around. Don't wander too far and get lost. Sharon, you and I will scout along the bank for berries and scan the water for fish.

Charlie and Sharon strolled slowly along the riverbank, brushing aside bushes, looking at the vegetation and into the water. Sharon knelt on a flat rock to cup some water in her hands. Before immersing her cupped hands, she stared into the river at, what appeared to be several sparkling pellets in the riverbed.

"Dad, come here. Look at this. What is it?"

Charlie knelt beside her. He reached down into the shallow water and brought out one of the small lumps. "Sharon, it's gold! That's a nugget of gold! I can see more. Reach in there and get as many as you can. This is an amazing find! There are probably more buried in the gravel at the bottom of the river. Grab as many as you can, and we'll show them to Tom and Jean."

"It's not pure gold, is it?"

"Oh no, there's other material in these nuggets. But there's quite a bit of gold here. Good, you've got several nuggets there. Let's go back to the falls."

3

GOLD

TOM DIDN'T SLEEP THAT NIGHT. Visions of gold nuggets raced through his mind. Thousand dollar bills were scattered among the nuggets. His imagination ran rampant. Where did they come from? Were there a lot more of them? What was it he had read about gold mining years ago? Oh yes, something about a mother lode. Somewhere, possibly nearby, was the source, the mother lode.

Rolling a nugget between his thumb and forefinger, he clutched the second nugget tightly in his other hand. Charlie and Sharon had given him the nuggets yesterday. He wondered how many Charlie had hidden for himself. Eager to begin searching for more gold, he impatiently waited for daylight. But an hour before sunrise his exhausted brain shut down as if a switch had been thrown, and he fell asleep.

Sharon was the first to wake up. After quietly preparing a fire and heating water for instant coffee, she went down to the river to wash her face. Gazing into the water, she couldn't help looking for more nuggets. There weren't any visible. She reached into her jeans pocket and brought out her two nuggets. Flashes of gold in the morning sun looked enticing.

Charlie and Jean joined her at the riverbank, paper cups of coffee in hand. "Good morning, Sharon," Charlie said. "Let's go hunting for berries and whatever else we can find to eat. We've got to find some food soon. Any more nuggets in there?"

"No, I can't see any. Is Tom still sleeping?"

"Like a baby," Jean said.

Tom's eyes suddenly popped open. The sun streaming onto his face glittered like gold. He sat up quickly and looked around. They were gone all three of them.

"Damn," he said to himself, "they're out there looking for gold." He sprinted past the fire and the boiling water with no thought of stopping for coffee. His only thought was of gold. There was no sign of his companions at the river. But he heard some bushes rustling downstream. He came upon them in the bushes picking currants.

"Hey, did you find any more gold?"

"Good morning, Tom. We're collecting something more important than gold, a bit of breakfast," Jean advised.

"I'm not hungry," Tom said impatiently.

After eating several currants and looking for other berries, they trudged upstream toward their camp. Charlie stopped suddenly as the falls came into view. The other three continued on.

Charlie had seen something about the falls he hadn't noticed before. The fifty-foot cascade of water was all white and foamy except for a dark area just above where it fell onto the rocks before continuing down into the pool. Why isn't the entire face of the falls white and foamy? Could there be an undercut in the cliff behind the waterfall? Could the source of gold be there, behind the falls?

Charlie joined the others at the campfire as they finished their coffee and allotment of saltines. "I'm going hunting this morning, folks. We need some solid food. Berries and crackers aren't enough. I'll be gone for two or three hours. I'm hoping to bag a rabbit or a quail. While I'm gone, if you like, why don't you three go wading in the river and see if you can find any more gold nuggets."

"Yeah, good idea, Charlie," Tom confirmed quickly.

Sharon said, "That'll be fun. And we can wash off some of the dirt we've collected. Jean and I can bathe in the pool at the base of the falls if you, Tom, will stay downstream and not peek through the bushes."

"Tom wouldn't do that, would you?" Jean interjected.

"Of course not. I'll be too busy looking for gold."

"Okay," Charlie said. "When I get back with our dinner, I'll tell you where I think we should look for the source of the gold."

"The mother lode!" Tom gasped.

Charlie returned in a few hours with a feast for the four crash survivors, a rabbit he had bagged with his little pistol. As he approached, holding his prize high above his head, the three hungry people cheered and pranced around him. That evening they dined in style, savoring every bite.

"Charlie, what's your idea about finding the source of the gold? I can't wait to hear it," Tom asked.

"We'll talk tomorrow morning, Tom. I'm worn out after hiking through the woods to get our dinner. I'm hitting my pine bough sack."

THE UNDERCUT

The next morning after their usual meager breakfast, Charlie announced, "Yesterday, I noticed a dark area in the waterfall, just above the rocks. Today, I'm going to climb up there and see what's behind the waterfall. I think there might be a cave or an undercut that causes that dark shadow in the water spray. Tom, you come with me. Ladies, you go pick some more berries."

"Right on, Charlie." Tom nearly roared.

"Dad, you be careful on those wet, slippery rocks. You too, Tom."

Charlie and Tom went down to the river a few feet from the waterfall where Charlie pointed out the dark spot in the falls. "I've looked at the terrain on both sides of the cliff there at the waterfall, and it looks like we can get to the ledge that goes behind the falls without crossing the river. We'll need to scramble up through those trees near the water. I'll lead the way, Tom. You follow me. Watch your step, especially on those slippery rocks."

"Okay, Charlie."

As they came out of the trees at the edge of the water Charlie was surprised to find the ledge a level pathway into the space behind the falls. It minimized the danger of slipping and falling.

"Tom, you wait here until I get under the falls and see what's back there. I'll signal you to come if it looks safe. Watch me to see how to get in there safely."

"You sound like an old hand at exploring."

Charlie stepped out of the trees onto the two-foot wide ledge and slowly walked forward, looking for handholds on the wall of the cliff. There were very few niches in the cliff wall. He edged along the path with the palms of his hands against the wall. The path was smooth and slick. After about ten feet he started to go behind the falling water. A misty spray fell lightly on him.

A few steps behind the waterfall Charlie came to the edge of a cutout in the cliff as he expected. Sunlight didn't penetrate far into the opening which made it difficult to see how deep it was. Holding on to the rock wall with his right hand, he pulled a flashlight out of his pocket and aimed its beam into the opening. It revealed a cave roughly thirty feet deep, seven feet wide, and about eight feet high.

He turned to Tom and yelled, "Come on, Tom. Slowly and carefully." Even over the noise of the waterfall, Tom heard the command and started forward. As he approached Charlie, one foot slipped on the sleek, wet path. Tom shouted an oath and grabbed Charlie's arm. It was enough to steady him. "I told you to go slow. Look past me, Tom. You can see where the ledge ends. This is the only way into the cave. Come on. Follow me."

They cautiously entered the cave, the flashlight giving them ample light. Charlie aimed its beam on the wall to their right as they walked slowly toward the back of the cave. About fifteen feet into the cave, Charlie stopped and gazed at the wall, shining the light at shoulder level. He went closer to inspect the wall.

"Tom, look at this. It's a vein of gold."

"Wow! We're rich, Charlie. Rich, rich! But how do we get it out?"

"Don't get too excited, Tom. Look closely. See those smooth marks on the wall. This gold has been discovered before. Those are the marks of a pickax."

"Maybe since they quit working the vein, it's only fools gold."

"Don't think so. I'll try to pry out a piece with my knife. Hold the flashlight." Charlie put the knifepoint in a crack and easily pried loose a two-inch chunk of rock stained with gold. "Come on, Tom. Let's check the other side and get out of here." The other side showed no evidence of gold. Leaving the cave, they slowly edged their way along the dangerous ledge and back into the trees.

Eager to spread the news, Tom said, "Come on, Charlie, let's tell the ladies. They'll flip."

THE CACHE

Eager to see the source of the gold nuggets, Sharon and Jean wanted to go to the cave immediately.

"Okay, but you have to be very careful walking the ledge behind the waterfall. It's wet and slippery," Charlie cautioned. "Come on. Follow me. Tom, you bring up the rear."

Charlie paused when they reached the ledge beside the waterfall. "Now, ladies, face the rock wall and put your hands on it like this." Charlie faced the wall and showed them what he meant. "Step sideways along the ledge, keeping your hands flat on the wall for balance. Follow me." One by onc, they edged their way to the opening of the cave behind the waterfall. Stepping into the cave, Charlie turned on the flashlight.

"Good thing you have a flashlight, Dad. It's really dark in here."

"Where is this fabulous treasure?" Jean queried.

Charlie moved halfway into the cave and over to the wall on the right. "Look where I'm pointing the light. What do you see?"

Sharon and Jean leaned forward expectantly. "It glitters like, like gold. Good Lord, it is gold there in the rock," Sharon gasped.

"So this is the mother lode. Looks like a lot of gold in that rock wall. And it shines more in some places," Jean observed.

Tom quickly said, "That's where a pickax has been used on the wall. This gold has been found before. Charlie, how long ago do you think it was originally discovered?"

"I don't know, Tom. But the fact that there's still a lot of gold here makes me think it may have been a long time ago and that whoever found it never came back to work his rich find."

"But, Dad, it could also mean that the person who found it left only recently and hasn't gotten back yet to work the mine."

"Sharon's got a point there," Jean blurted out.

Tom came forward. "Charlie, shine the light toward the back of the cave. Let's see what's there."

They all cautiously walked toward the innermost recess of the cave, their light illuminating an odd pile of rocks at the far end. It didn't look like a natural formation of rocks they seemed to have been deliberately piled there.

"What have we here?" Charlie said thoughtfully. "These look like stones from the river. They're not natural cave rock. Looks like they've been piled here by human hands."

Tom kneeled down and started pulling rocks from the pile. After a couple of minutes, he stopped. "Wow! Look at this. Chunks of rock filled with gold! The guy that found these must have stashed them here, intending to come back for them. Wow!"

"Looks like you're right, Tom. Pull a few more rocks off and see what else is in there."

"There must be a fortune in gold there," Jean said, "and even more still in the cave wall."

Tom worked fast, scattering loose rocks around the floor of the cave. "Look here's the pickax. It must be the one he used to dig out the gold. And look, here's a carbide lamp."

"Let me see it," Charlie asked quickly. Tom handed it to Charlie. After examining it closely Charlie tossed it back on the pile. "Come on. We've got to get out of here. We can't use up all of our flashlight batteries in here. We've seen enough. Come on. Sharon, you go first. Tom, you next, and stay close to her. Jean, you next, and I'll stay close to you. Remember, stay close to the wall on the ledge and don't hurry."

As they slowly edged along the path, Jean's foot slipped on the wet surface. She screamed as she started to fall. Charlie's arm instantly shot out and grabbed her arm. He pulled her back up onto the ledge next to him and held her tight. She was panting and terrified. "It's okay, Jean. You're okay. I'll hang on to you the rest of the way. Slowly now. One step at a time. We're almost to the end of the ledge and into the trees."

Jean collapsed at the end of the ledge, sobbing now that her ordeal was over. Charlie and Sharon kneeled beside her and tried to calm her. They returned to their campsite, Jean supported on Charlie's arm. After sitting down a few minutes to calm themselves and gather their thoughts, Charlie said, "Are you all right, Jean? I hope I didn't hurt your arm."

"I'm okay. Thanks, Charlie. I would have gone right over the falls into the pool. If I hadn't hit any rocks on the way down, that is. Oh God."

Changing the subject, Charlie said, "Now folks, that pickax we found it's an old one. I've seen one like it on display at the museum in Cripple Creek. Gold was discovered in that area in the 1800s, you know. The antique pickax could mean our gold was discovered long ago by a prospector who found the cave and the gold but never got back to stake his claim. Who knows what happened to him. Maybe a bear got him, maybe the Indians. We'll probably never know. So, I think we're the only people who know about this rich vein of gold."

"That's good news. It's all ours," Tom chortled.

Jean interrupted saying, "There's bad news too, Tom. Do you know how heavy gold is? How are we going to get it out of here? Charlie says we have about a thirty-mile hike. You could carry two pockets full of gold nuggets, and even at that, you'd have a hard time. Charlie, do you have any ideas? This has become intriguing to me. It seems like our problems are overwhelming."

Charlie yawned and said, "Let's sleep on it. Try not to let the glitter of gold keep you awake tonight. We'll address our most important problems survival and walking out of here tomorrow. I'm bushed. Good night. Don't let the gold bug bite."

"Very funny," Tom chided. "I want that gold. Let's figure a way to get it out."

"Quiet Good night."

"Tom," Jean whispered, "come with me. Bring your coat." Quietly they walked out of the little clearing and into the woods.

THE GLADE

Jean led Tom along the riverbank a little ways before she stopped, turned, and kissed him passionately.

"Tom, you've got gold fever, and I have just the cure for it. There's a little hidden glade nearby where we can be alone and undisturbed. Just look at the moon, all those sparkling stars, and me. Doesn't all this make you think of something other than gold?"

"Jean, you're a clever little lady. If your cure is what I think it is, I'm your man."

"You know the treatment I can give you, and I need something from you too. Come. Let me show you a place I found when I was looking for berries."

She turned away from the river and pushed through the brush into the thickly wooded forest. The full moon helped to light their way as they continued on to what appeared to be a solid wall of bushes. Jean circled to the right and pushed through them into a small clearing, walled with bushes and tree trunks.

"Here is our trysting place. Isn't it lovely? I feel like that summer moonlight filtering through the trees is telling us to make love."

"This is a wonderful place. The pine fragrance is inviting. And you, you are even more inviting."

"Yes, the sweet scent of wildflowers sets the scene for me to cure your fever and for you to satisfy my hunger."

It was almost a contest to see who could get out of their clothes first. The urgency, expectation, was powerful and demanding. Jean, the winner, crouched over Tom as he fell back on their mattress of clothes. She kissed him hungrily and noting his immediate response moved her lips to his neck, chest, and on down to his rigidity. Tom moaned with pleasure as he watched her in the moonlight. Thoughts of gold vanished.

She lay down beside him. "Now, Tom," she urged. "Give me the treatment, as only you can do."

Silently he kissed her and then traversed her body with his lips, knowing it would bring her to a complete frenzy of passion. Tingling nipples on her beautiful breasts hardened as he kissed and sucked. When he reached her stomach she cried, "Oh, Tom. Now! I need you. Now, please."

They reached the pinnacle of passion at the same time and groans of ecstasy filled their private glade. Spent bodies and gasps testified to the satiation that engulfed them. Cooling off, they dressed, and headed back to camp.

4

THE LONG MILES

CHARLIE WOKE UP JUST AS THE SUN APPEARED between the mountain peaks, erasing the deep gloom in the forest. His thoughts immediately turned to their predicament. As pilot and leader of the group, the responsibility to shepherd his marooned passengers safely back to civilization was his primary concern. He moved about, taking deep gulps of the crisp mountain air, determined to keep his mind clear.

Last night, unable to sleep, he sat before the fire working and reworking his plans. Even when he tried to sleep, he could not stop thinking about their dilemma. Their hike out would begin soon. Fortunately, the weather was perfect for a long trek through the forest.

Scanning his sleeping survivors, alternately scowling and smiling, he made coffee. His thoughts whirled about like clouds caught in a storm current, the unavoidable crash, their isolation, the daunting dangers ahead. And yes, even the gold was a problem. Discovering it was their good fortune, but getting it out could be hell. He swallowed a bit of coffee, choking on the first hot sip. His priority was to get them all out of here safely and as quickly as possible.

"C'mon gang, up, up. Let's get going. We've lots of scenery to admire and miles to go."

Jean roused herself from her makeshift sleeping bag of clothes. "Oh, Charlie, it seems like I just got to sleep. It's barely light," she pouted, sitting up, shivering a little. Resigning herself to the task ahead, she smiled a greeting. "So, good morning."

Charlie met her glance with pursed lips that seemed to signal yet suppress an emotional challenge. "Well, good morning to you, Jean. It won't be long until the sun will shine through those trees to warm us up, and you'll welcome this new day. The sooner we get started, the sooner we'll get to hot showers and steak dinners. Coffee's ready."

Scowling, Tom sat up. "What about the gold? What do we do about that leave a bonanza behind?"

"How did I guess that would be your first concern this morning?" Charlie gritted his teeth, determined not to lose his temper. "Well, Tom, maybe for a time we may have to do just that. Look, we all want the gold. But let's face it, we have a long, dangerous trek ahead, and even gold can become a heavy burden, especially if we have climbing to do."

Charlie's voice rose as his eyes followed Tom stepping away for a quick stop behind a tree. In minutes he was back, adjusting his zipper.

"Hell, Charlie, I don't see why we can't take some along! It's unreasonable to leave so much behind," he grumbled.

Charlie scowled, shaking his head. "Keeping us all alive and getting us to safety is my main concern. But I'm no fool, we're not forgetting about the gold."

"Dad, couldn't we take along, say, just a pocketful?" Sharon coaxed.

"Okay, but only that much, not too heavy. Remember, we have miles to go, and if you add on a heavy load of gold, you'll find yourself chucking it and no way to find it later."

Jean listened, sipping her coffee, ruefully examining her hands. "Oh, what I wouldn't do for a beauty parlor and a manicure," she sighed, reaching for a damp cracker, "and maybe a nice buttery croissant." She ran her fingers through her short dark locks, annoyed by the coarse, dirty feel of it. "Charlie, I get the idea that you, we'll be coming back here? Are you catching gold fever too? How on earth could we get the gold out of here?"

"Yes Dad, how can we possibly do that."

"I don't know. But first we have to get to Montrose. I know which direction to take. Unfortunately, we have to walk. Start rolling up your gear while I talk."

Grumbling, Tom made sure he stayed within earshot.

"First, we all swear to silence. Once we're out of here, no one talks about it to anyone. This is just between us. Agreed?" Satisfied as they vigorously nodded, Charlie stomped the fire out, covering it with dirt. "And then there's the money we'll need, money to make it back here with a helicopter."

"Hey, wait, wait," Tom grimaced, his hand raised in protest. "Take it easy. When, and if, we make our way out, what makes you think we can find our way back to the gold in this wild country, this wilderness?"

"I'll find it all right. I've made my calculations. If I'm correct about the direction to Montrose, then I'm confident we can find our way back here. Remember, we're only a little way from Ohio Peak.

"I still wanna fill my pockets," Tom complained, turning to the two women for agreement.

"Drink your coffee, Tom," Jean admonished mildly. "We've got to get going."

"The pockets of my jeans aren't very roomy, but I'm going to squeeze a few nuggets into them," Sharon giggled, sensing the growing tension.

"Look, I don't want to be a mean bastard or make things difficult. On the contrary, I'm only thinking about the difficulty of the hike ahead of us. We might even have to chuck some of our belongings along the way, it could come to that. So, make your choice, gold, or what's really necessary. What you take, you carry. And don't forget gold is very heavy."

Sharon picked up her small bundle, gesturing to her father to tie it on her back, holding out for all to see the few nuggets she put into her pockets.

Jean opened a small purse revealing several gold nuggets. "For a necklace, just to remember this, ah, good time." She looked up at Charlie, smiling whimsically. "When you said we'll need money to make it back here, what did you have in mind?"

"A helicopter. A big one. We can't rent or lease one. If word got out about this, we'd be dealing with a gold rush to rival the one in California in 1849. Somehow, we must manage to get one on the sly. And we'll need other supplies."

"I don't want to make rash promises, but if we get out, I may be able to handle buying it. Let me know what kind of chopper we need and how much it costs," Jean said.

"We'll get out of here. Don't you worry. And we'll all share in the cost eventually, if you understand me."

"Sure, Charlie, the money from the gold." Jean smiled. "Well, I'm ready to move out," she nearly shouted, "but I do wish we had either wheels or wings."

Charlie winked at her and smiled. "Angels don't need wings."

THE BROWN PERIL

The four hikers struggled up a steep slope in the forest, Tom bringing up the rear. Looking up, he thought he saw gold in the trees. Quickly discerning it was just the sun glistening on shiny leaves, he murmured, "Damn, I really must have gold fever."

In front of Tom, Jean trudged up the slope doggedly, breathing hard. Quietly, she said to herself, please give me strength. Please, Lord, help us get out of here.

Charlie, in the lead, stopped abruptly. He turned slowly and gestured with his hands for the others to stop. "Don't move and don't make any noise," he whispered.

The three tired travelers wondered at his sudden authoritative order, but complied.

Charlie slowly looked up over his shoulder to the crest of the slope, peering intently at the trees and bushes. He turned again to his companions and quietly warned, "Stand very still and don't make any noise. We have a problem up ahead. Tom, come slowly, no noise, here to me."

Charlie looked up the slope again, then turned back to face his charges. Whispering, he said, "Look at the largest pine tree on the left, at the top of the hill directly in front of us. See the brown bear near the trunk of the tree? Quiet now!" They all focused on the big tree at the top of the hill.

The huge bear was staring directly down the slope at them, not moving a muscle. Suddenly there was movement in the bushes near the bear. Charlie noticed it first and knew immediately that it was a bear cub.

"No noise, folks. Our problem has just escalated. That bear has a cub with her. She's even more dangerous, protecting her cub."

"Dad," Sharon whispered, "shouldn't we go back down the hill and get out of here."

"No, we stay right here and don't move. Brown bears, by nature, are not aggressive, but with her cub nearby we have to be very careful. We mustn't do anything that threatens her, and we must never get between her and the cub. She'll charge us if we do."

"But how long do we have to stay here," Tom asked nervously.

"Yes, how long do we stand here motionless," Jean added.

"Sorry," Charlie replied, "we have to wait until mama bear decides to leave with her cub. She has to know that we're not a threat. If you get tired, sit down slowly, one at a time. I'd guess in about fifteen minutes she'll decide it's safe to amble off into the forest. Don't worry, we'll be okay if you all just stay still and don't make any noise."

Jean slowly sat on a nearby log and Sharon joined her. Charlie and Tom remained standing.

The standoff lasted a few more minutes before the bear and her cub finally turned back into the forest, mama bear giving them one last look and a quiet growl.

Charlie said, "We should wait five minutes before moving on out of here. The bear angled off to our right, so we'll go left. Now, just be patient and quiet."

Slowly and warily they climbed to the top of the hill, always looking to their right. Charlie led them down the other side of the hill, away from the bear, away from danger.

After walking another hour, they came upon a small clearing.

"Here's our camp for tonight," Charlie advised. "I see some good berry bushes. Pick some while I go hunting. With luck I'll bring back an enticing entree for our dinner. Don't wander off too far. Build a small fire. I'll try to be back within the hour."

After a few tasty berries and a sip of water, Charlie strode off in the direction of their objective, the town of Maher. He walked slowly and quietly, eyes alert for any movement. Twenty minutes into his search he came to a small pond; a collection basin for mountain run-off water. From the cover of trees he saw a deer drinking from the pond. The buck was too big and too far away for his thirty-eight pistol to bring down, but nearer to Charlie, a duck was paddling slowly across the pond. Charlie took aim, leaning against a tree to steady himself. Not willing to chance wasting a bullet, he waited patiently for the duck to stop. It wasn't a long wait, Charlie fired.

The noise of the shot caused the deer to bolt into the forest and disappear. Charlie's aim was true, the duck slumped over in the water. Retrieving his prize, Charlie immediately dressed it out in preparation for cooking. His fellow travelers would savor a delicious duck dinner.

The crack of a twig brought Charlie's head up quickly in the direction of the sound. At the same time he changed the knife to his left hand and drew the pistol from his pocket. At the edge of the forest, about fifty feet away, he saw two shining fiery eyes staring at him. At that instant a mountain lion charged him.

Charlie had time for only one thought, *he's not getting our dinner*, and fired straight and quick. The beast sprang at him as he fired. Charlie swiftly dove away from his attacker, but too late to avoid the claws that raked his left arm from elbow to wrist as the lion fell dead at his feet. Arm bleeding profusely from the deep slashes and groaning with pain, Charlie rose from the ground beside the dead mountain lion. *Got to stop the bleeding*, he thought. He pulled the large kerchief from his pocket and wrapped it tightly around his arm, applying pressure with his right hand. He held his arm upright to stem the flow of blood. As he sat there, his mind swirling, he reached for the duck and vowed to get back to camp with it. His kerchief was soaked with blood. Use your undershirt, he told his fuzzy brain.

After a struggle, able to use only his right arm, Charlie pulled the top of his flight suit down and the undershirt off. He quickly wrapped his left arm and stood up, keeping his injured arm up across his chest. His pistol back in his pocket, he picked up the knife and the duck, and headed back into the forest. I need the first aid kit, and I've got to get back to my Sharon, Jean, and Tom. He plodded on, fighting dizziness, stumbling, and walking as fast as he was able.

CHARLIE'S FIRST AID

"Dad, what happened," Sharon cried as she saw Charlie stumble from the forest, still clutching the duck. "Oh God, your arm, it's all bloody," she screamed. "Jean, get the first aid kit."

"Yes, first aid kit," Charlie implored as he crawled to a tree and leaned back against it. "Sharon, here's tonight's dinner."

Returning with the kit, Jean asked,"Oh, Charlie, how did you get hurt?" A look of concern on her face.

"Big cat jumped me," Charlie gasped, his face pale as he closed his eyes. His lips were turning blue, and his breathing was labored.

Sharon opened the kit and brought out a large bandage and a box of four-by-four sterile gauze pads. "We've got to get this blood-soaked rag off before the blood dries or we'll reopen the wounds. Jean, heat some water."

Sharon slowly unwound the soaked undershirt. "Easy, Dad. We'll fix you up. Try to relax."

Charlie winced as Sharon pulled off the blood-soaked undershirt. Her eyes narrowed when she saw the three deep gashes in her father's arm. She opened the bottle of peroxide and poured some on the wounds. It bubbled and fizzed, cleaning the wounds. Placing several of the large bandage pads on his arm she applied pressure to stop the bleeding.

Tom, building up the fire, muttered to Jean, "Now there's two of us walking wounded. Hope you ladies stay healthy."

Jean mumbled agreement as she heated water. After applying

pressure on Charlie's arm for two minutes, Sharon removed the bandages and was relieved to see the bleeding had stopped. She patted the wounds dry.

"Dad, how do you feel now? We're cooking the duck. Doesn't it smell delicious? Want some water or a cup of coffee?"

"I'll be okay. I'm not dizzy any more. And that roast duck, even without l'orange, will restore me as much as your nursing my arm did. And yes, coffee."

Sharon found the steri-strips and with Jean's help, closed the gashes. Then she firmly wrapped the arm with a clean bandage. "Dad, keep your arm above the level of your heart for a few more minutes so it doesn't start bleeding again."

After the feast of roast duck, the last rays of sun filtered through the trees announcing it was time to rest, to sleep. Charlie told them about his encounter with the mountain lion.

"You know, mountain lions don't distinguish between humans, deer, or elk. Evidently, I came upon this one at the wrong time, when she was in hunting mode. So she went for me. Fortunately, I was quick enough with my pistol. Now I have to get some sleep. We'll get an early start tomorrow. There isn't far to go, maybe only another day or two. Get your rest." Charlie fell asleep immediately.

Morning arrived with dark clouds, threatening rain. With no sunlight to waken them, the weary four slept on, losing their chance to get an early start. After savoring the last of their crackers with coffee and making their necessary ablutions, they continued their pilgrimage to civilization. Charlie seemed as strong as ever, plunging ahead with his compass. Sharon had put his arm in a sling to protect it. But the rigors of slogging through the forest and inadequate food were showing. Their pace had slowed.

They passed the body of the dead mountain lion and paused there to fill their water jug from the pond and rest a while. The day wore on, and by nightfall they were hungry and exhausted but were still not out of the forest.

"Cheer up, folks. We'll be out of this wilderness tomorrow. We can look forward to a shower, a steak, and a stiff drink soon," Charlie pledged.

5

OUT OF THE WILDERNESS

LAGGING BEHIND CHARLIE THE NEXT DAY, Jean paused in alarm when she saw him stop abruptly. Holding up one hand to signal the others to halt, he cupped the other to his ear.

"So, what is it, Charlie?" she puffed as she caught up with him, pushing back her tousled hair.

"Look, light ahead, that's what," he gestured with new enthusiasm. "Light and no trees. And listen, do you hear something familiar? Like the sound of a car in the distance?"

"Sound, noise? What are you talking about?" Lathered with perspiration, Tom shuffled up impatiently. "For all we know, we've been going in circles."

Charlie grimaced but ignored Tom's gloomy remark. "Well, Tom, if you listen carefully for a minute with your mouth shut, you'll hear the sound of a car. I heard a truck off in the distance too. That means people, civilization. It means finally out of the woods, a decent meal, a shower, and all that good stuff."

"I'll take your word for it. I'm too pooped to cheer, but am I glad we made it," he wheezed. "God, I thought we'd never get out of those woods."

Sharon caught up with her father. Hugging him, she looked up with loving eyes at the sorely tired, older man, who at that moment felt a new vitality and an overwhelming sense of accomplishment. It was a victory. Much like Lewis and Clark must have felt, he thought. Like them, he had led his bedraggled band to safety.

Wearily, Jean managed her congratulations with a warm smile. "I knew you could do it, Charlie. I never had any doubt. Now let's head for civilization. Oh, for a bubble bath! And a beauty salon."

"Dad, you've done it! You saved us," Sharon continued to hug her father. Her nose wrinkled up as she pulled away. "But oh, Dad, you, all of us need a shower!" She turned to Jean. "I'm a mess. Tell me, do I look as bad as I feel?"

"At your age, darling," Jean admonished good-naturedly, "a pretty girl like you is never a mess. It's us older broads that need the attention." Jean patted Sharon's cheek affectionately. "But I'll see that we get the best available, sweetie."

Sharon pointed to her father's arm. "Jean, first thing is to get Dad to a doctor for that arm!" Jean nodded, hugging the younger girl. "I'm worried too. First thing."

As they ventured beyond the edge of the forest, Charlie turned to caution them again. "Remember, not a word about the gold and keep those nuggets out of sight."

With renewed vigor they almost trotted past a field skirting the forest, beyond which they could see a narrow road. A small gas station was visible where the road curved into the distance, probably a one-pump mom and pop operation. Beyond it they could make out a motel sign. To the weary group it was as welcome as the Ritz Carlton. It meant food, running water, communication, and above all, safety. After six days of struggling through the wilderness they had reached safety.

"Seems to me this could be the outskirts of Maher," Charlie observed thoughtfully, peering intently into the distance, watching as a small farm truck faded into the horizon. "We'll get rooms, have a big dinner, and sleep comfortably for a change."

"Not before we find a doctor," his daughter insisted.

"Sure, that too." Her father nodded. "First, I'll have to call Jake back in Denver to let everyone know we're okay. I'll have him notify the FAA so they can call off the search, if they haven't already."

The proprietor of the motel had heard about the airplane crash and the missing pilot and passengers that had by now been given up for lost. He was eager to help, and after providing rooms, he drove Charlie to the medical center in town. When they returned to the motel, the local press, alerted by the medical facility, was already waiting for interviews. Fortunately, Tom and the women were not available. They were sound asleep.

Charlie spoke briefly to the reporters and promised to give them a more detailed story in the morning. The owner of the motel, glad of the unexpected publicity, offered everyone free drinks in the small bar, allowing Charlie to get to his room. After a quick shower and shave, he sat down on the bed and fell asleep as soon as his head hit the pillow.

He was awakened by someone nudging him gently. Not quite morning, a faint gray haze showed through the window of the small, simply furnished room.

Looking up, he saw Jean sitting on the bed.

"The connecting door wasn't locked, so I walked in. Sharon and I are sharing the room next to you. She's sound asleep. Tom is down the hall. I guess he's still asleep too. But I had to stay awake until you returned." She smiled apologetically. "So, how's the arm?"

"Not too bad. Guess I'll live," he joked. He sat up, turning around to face Jean. "I never thought about reporters. I guess we'll just have to face the cameras, get it over with..."

"I'm afraid so—but publicity might cause us problems."

Charlie hesitated, getting the sleep out of his brain. "Oh, you mean the, uh, shiny stuff!" He grinned. "Yes. We'll need to be careful talking to reporters about our what happened in the forest. Remind Sharon, no mention of the gold."

"And Tom? Think he'll shoot off his mouth?"

"I don't think so. He's too greedy, but I'll talk to him in the morning."

"It is morning."

"Nobody else is up."

"Then I'll go back to bed. I just wanted to make sure you were all right. I was worried."

"I'm flattered. You're sweet, you know."

"No one's called me sweet since I was in high school."

"Then no one knows what you're really like," Charlie said as he reached for her hand. "I'm looking forward to getting together when we get back to Denver."

"Yes, I am too."

Before breakfast, a sleepy Tom answered Charlie's insistent knocking on his bedroom door. Scratching his head, obviously annoyed, he focused his gaze on Charlie. "You up already? Dressed and ready to go where?"

"No, Tom, we're not ready to go yet. There are reporters around with a camera crew. I just came to remind you not to say a word about that " Charlie said, pointing to a gold nugget shining on the night table beside the window. "Put that away, Tom, and keep it put away. Word'll get out."

Tom shuffled over and dropped it into the pocket of the jacket he wore while in the forest. "Just wanted to look at it, y'know."

"Keep it out of sight. There are press people in the lobby. That's all we need, so be prepared. We're expecting a limousine here at ten to take us to the local airport about twelve miles from here. I've already arranged for a small plane to fly us to Denver. Once we get there, we can make plans. Meanwhile, Tom, watch what you say."

Tom eyed him suspiciously. "Of course. I expect we'll all stay together until then, especially since we've all become such good friends," he said snidely.

Charlie assessed Tom critically. Trouble, he thought, this man means trouble. He shook his head, his deep-set blue eyes thoughtful and concerned. "If you're worried about us, put it out of your mind. I speak for my daughter and for Jean as well."

6

CHARLIE AND JEAN

TWO DAYS AFTER THEY RETURNED to Denver, Charlie told his three partners about the call from the FAA. That agency wanted to find the crashed aircraft to determine what caused the loss of oil. They needed to know if the problem was caused by a defect that could be fixed. Charlie had given the coordinates to the FAA supervisor. He told his companions they'd have to wait a while before returning to the waterfall. But that wasn't a problem because they needed time to plan their expedition to the mother lode. Charlie gave Jean the task of searching the library for information on the technicalities of filing for and recording a claim.

While the FAA was searching for the crashed Arrow, Jean spent hours at the Denver main library. Charlie checked on the availability of helicopters. Sharon and Tom were kept busy at work.

After ten days of research, Jean called Charlie. "I've finished my work at the library. When can we get together?"

"Anytime this weekend is fine with me. I presume Sharon and Tom will be available. We can meet at my house. Why don't you call Tom to see if eight o'clock Saturday evening is okay. I'll check with Sharon. Okay?"

"Okay, but I'd like to talk it over with you first. Could we get together sometime before Saturday? We could have a drink and enjoy an evening out too."

"I have a better idea. Let's go to my favorite bistro for dancing and drinks and leave out any talk of gold hunting.

"Charlie, I'd love that. Pleasure before business is a marvelous idea."

"How about me picking you up in my MG at seven on Friday. Perhaps we can put that whole adventure out of our minds temporarily and just have a good time getting to know one another better, etc."

"Hmm. Wonder what the etc. part is?"

"Hopefully, we'll find out."

At Charlie's favorite bar and lounge they sipped their drinks and indulged in idle chitchat, avoiding the subject of gold. It was difficult. Even Charlie had a hard time not talking about it. They danced to slow music, finding mysterious excitement in each other's eyes. Jean melted against Charlie as they flowed smoothly over the dance floor.

When they sat down, Charlie felt compelled to ask, "Jean, what's your tie to Tom?"

"He's just an occasional companion. I enjoy his company, but there's nothing serious between us. How about you? Any, ah, companions?"

"Only my airplane. But she's gone now. She's been my only concern other than my daughter. Jean, I'm worried about Tom. You know him better than I do. Do you think he'll be a problem in any way?"

"He's a sort of Jekyl and Hyde. He can be charming at times. Other times he can sort of explode. He's money hungry and would do almost anything to get it. I know because he's been after me to marry him, but I suspect my money is the main attraction. I think I can handle him, keep him under control. Between the two of us, we should be able keep him reined in. Right?"

"I guess knowing his shortcomings, you'll be able to head off any problems he might start causing. Okay! Now, how would you like a guided tour of my hangar office? It's more than just an office. Sometimes I stay there overnight. It's nothing fancy. You might even consider it rustic. I'm sure it's nothing like what you're used to, but there's a bottle of Haig and Haig there and for you, a bottle of Harpers. How does that sound?"

"I was hoping you would suggest something like that. I know

what rustic is, Charlie, my dear. Some day I'll tell you how. I haven't always been a rich bitch. Let's go."

Charlie opened his office door and Jean entered first. It was a total surprise to her. She expected a typical man's messy room, but on Charlie's desk the papers were arranged in neat piles. A small bookshelf filled with aircraft manuals and FAA regulation books was as orderly as a rank of cadets ready for inspection. The large old-fashioned desk and matching chair were in perfect condition, and the ancient leather armchair in front of the desk was equally impressive. Pictures of airplanes decorated the walls. On the desk was one picture, a picture of his daughter.

Jean's eyes focused on a door at one end of the room. A sign attached to the door read, "R & R Room".

"Charlie, I really don't need another Harper's. What's the R & R room?"

"Just as advertised, the rest and relaxation room, my sanctum sanctorum, my retreat, my hideaway. It's where I go to get rid of troubling thoughts, to solve problems and be alone."

"Can I see it?"

"Of course, come."

Again Jean walked into an immaculate room. The bed was made, covered with a spread picturing an open-cockpit WACO airplane flying in a sky of blue over a field of red tulips. A small bureau and one ladder-back chair completed the furnishings. Adjoining the bedroom was a small, immaculate bathroom. "Charlie, how often do you stay here?"

"Once or twice a week, normally. But now that my Arrow is gone, I'm usually at home."

They sat on the bed and Charlie put his arm around Jean. She turned to him, took his face between her hands, and kissed him lightly. Charlie returned her kiss with a long passionate embrace. They both realized instinctively that making love was inevitable, inescapable.

Charlie marveled at Jean's flawless body. Paraphrasing one of Teddy Roosevelt's statements, he thought that adequately describing her would bankrupt the English language. She was beyond all praise. Jean glanced at Charlie as he undressed, unable to take his eyes off her. She could read his mind through his eyes and was pleased.

Expressing their frenzied passion with their bodies, there was no need for words. Afterwards, exhausted, they lay side-by-side, holding hands, whispering words of love until they fell asleep. They slept in each other's arms 'til dawn.

As she was leaving the next morning, Jean said, "Now I know what your 'etc.' means. I think you should rename your hangar bedroom 'The Etcetera Room'."

Charlie smiled and kissed her lightly.

HOW TO FILE A CLAIM

Charlie had an array of bottled spirits and mixes lined up on the buffet with bucket of ice. Coffee was ready, and the four crash survivors relaxed on comfortable chairs in the living room. An aura of cautious expectancy permeated the small talk as Charlie came in with his scotch and water.

"Well, now we take the next step in our quest for gold. The planning begins. Jean has compiled information on filing a claim, which we need to determine the feasibility of any plans we come up with. Jean, it's your turn in the spotlight."

"Okay. I've spent several hours at the library digging for the facts we need. Basically, it's all good news. I'll have to refer to my notes as I go along. The Congressional Act of 1872 is the basic law governing gold claims. Then the Mineral Leasing Act was passed in 1920. The latest regulation is in a Congressional Act of July 1955.

The critical thing is the category of the land we found the gold on. Colorado is a public-land state. Public land is divided into two categories, National Parks or Monuments, which is closed to prospecting, and National Forest land, which is open to prospecting for gold. Guess what? Our waterfall is in public land open to prospecting. That's the best news. Pardon me. Time out to fix another bourbon."

"Sounds like you delved deeply into the books, Jean," Charlie said, proud of her.

"But what's the bad news?" Tom questioned sourly.

"Relax, Tom. There's no bad news," Jean said.

Sharon got up to pour a cup of coffee. "Sounds encouraging."

They sipped their drinks. Glancing at her notes, Jean continued. "Now, how to file and stake claim. Our gold, a vein in rock, is called a lode, so we file a lode claim. There is also a placer claim, but we aren't concerned with that. Our lode claim will be a rectangular shape. Each corner of the rectangle must have a marker post, and there must be a post in the middle of each long side of the rectangle. The starting point is called the discovery shaft. In our case, it's the vein behind the waterfall. We specify the number of feet we want on each side of the discovery shaft. For example, we might specify fifty feet on each side, or perhaps the maximum area allowed. The length of the claim is determined by the general course of the lode as near as may be, according to the rule. For us, it could be from a hundred feet downstream to a few feet above the falls. Can you picture it in your mind?"

"Yes," Charlie said immediately.

"How far above the falls should we begin our claim, Dad?"

"Oh, I'd say thirty feet would be safe. No telling how far the vein goes, it might peter-out in two or three feet. But we don't want the labor and expense of blasting through rock to make a long tunnel. There's plenty of gold ore visible in the cut-out."

"I hope so," Tom said.

Jean continued. "To record our claim, the county recorder needs to know five things. First, our name for the lode. I thought of the name 'Arrow' for Charlie's airplane. Second, the name of the locator. In our case, the four of us. The third is the date of location, which is when we discovered it. Next, the number of feet claimed on each side of the discovery shaft. And finally, the general course of the lode, which I mentioned before. Another requirement is that we must spend at least one hundred dollars a year working the claim. This is called annual assessment work."

"Wow, what a stringent requirement—all of a hundred dollars," Tom chortled.

Jean went on. "Oh, I almost forgot. A lode claim can be as large as six hundred feet by fifteen hundred feet. Colorado requires an exact copy of a notice of the lode location be recorded within sixty days. Charlie, I think you'll be glad to hear this next item. Regulations allow us to clear timber for access to the claim site. So we can open up a place for our chopper to land."

"Hey, that is good news," Charlie said.

"The important thing is finding out what the ore is worth. From what I read, chipping out one-inch ore samples across the vein for a total weight of one to two pounds is recommended. Then we take the samples to the U.S. Bureau of Mines in Denver for a fire assay and weighing, which will tell us the value of the gold within the ore. Currently gold is valued at about $340.00 an ounce, but the market changes daily."

"One more thing, ownership of the claim area is secured by a patent. This requires a survey, proof of expenditure of five hundred dollars, and payment to the U.S. Government of $2.50 per acre. But we don't have to get a patent because a valid location claim and assessment holds a mining claim indefinitely. Most of this information comes from a 1961 book titled *Successful Mineral Collecting and Prospecting*. So there it is. How to file a claim and so forth."

"Jean, you've done a marvelous job. We appreciate it," Charlie said gratefully.

"Yes, absolutely. Right, Tom?" Sharon agreed.

"Of course. Thanks, Jean."

They all fixed themselves another drink as Charlie began his report. "I've been checking on the availability and capability of various helicopters and found two choppers that can do our job. One is the Boeing Vertol Model 114, which can carry a 25,000-pound load, has a service ceiling of 15,000 feet, and a range of 242 miles. The other is a Boeing Model 234 with similar capabilities. I don't have prices on purchasing or leasing yet, but I should have those numbers by next week. Then we can decide how to go, Jean. I have a chopper pilot friend who'll be available. Jake, my mechanic, and another guy I know will do the heavy work like felling trees, clearing, and digging "One more thing. I expect to hear from the FAA investigators in about a week. I'll call all of you to set up our next meeting when I have more information. Have another drink, and then let's call it an evening."

As the others finished their drinks, Jean sipped hers slowly and lingered

"Charlie, I have to talk to you. Not about last night, although our etc. was wonderful. I've been doing some serious thinking. You know, I can easily finance our project at the waterfall, the Arrow claim. And I want to do it. But there's something else I'd also like to do. It's obvious to me that one of life's joys for you is flying. Now that you've been deprived of your pride and joy, your airplane, I'd like to get you another one."

"Jean , I..."

"Wait. It's not just because I can afford to buy an airplane, it's because I would get as much pleasure from giving as you would get from having your own airplane again. Please Charlie, let me do this."

"Jean, I'm astonished. This is like a bolt out of the blue. But I'm going to surprise you by not acting like one of those macho guys who says, 'I can't let you do this, somehow I'll get an airplane myself.' I accept your generous offer."

Jean pressed against him and cooed, "Thank you. You've made me very happy."

"You're thanking me. Jean, I can't thank you enough. Would you like to hear about what has been, up to now, only a dream? I don't want another Arrow. I want a plane strictly for fun. I've had enough of ferrying passengers around the country. My new plane would be a personal flying machine, just room for me and one other person. Can you guess what it would be?"

"Hmm...I just might know. Can I ask one question before answering?"

"Only one."

"Is it an old type of airplane?"

"Yes."

"Okay, I don't know what it's called, but it's the one pictured on your R & R room bedspread."

"You're so perceptive. You are absolutely right. It's an open cockpit, bi-wing airplane called the WACO, dating back to the twenties. Nowadays, one has to buy a replica. I don't know what they cost, could be a hundred thousand dollars. That's the toy I'd love to fly. And Jean, you'd be in the front, and I'd fly it from the rear cockpit."

"Consider it a done deal, Charlie, and I'd love to be with you the first flight."

"Done."

INTO THE CLOUDS OF ECSTACY

Charlie leaned back in his office chair at the hangar. He put his feet up on the desk and looked at the pictures of airplanes on the walls. His gaze focused on the picture of a WACO. *Man,* he thought, *I'm sure going to love having that plane*. Still staring at the WACO, his thoughts turned to Jean. He saw the plane with his eyes, but visions of Jean filled his mind.

What does she see in that klutz, Tom? I wonder if she goes out with other guys from her upper crust crowd. With all that money she must have plenty of guys on the string. So how come she latched on to me? Of course, it could be a one-time fling, but maybe she'll go out with me again. She seems to really like me. The WACO seemed to dissolve before his eyes, he saw only Jean. I'll call her.

"Hello, Jean. Charlie, your pilot and guide here."

"Oh, Charlie. I know you by your deep, sexy voice. It's nice to hear from my pilot and guide as you say. What's going on?"

"I'd like to update you on progress so far on the helicopter and check out an idea with you. Can we get together?"

"Sure! Come over to my house, and I'll fix us drinks. I'd sure like to hear your new idea."

"I'll be there in a half hour."

Jean met Charlie at the door with a scotch and water and led him to the sofa where her drink was waiting.

"Thanks for the quick scotch."

"It's one of your favorites, Haig and Haig."

"I've got a line on a Vertol helicopter we can lease. It'll cost about two thousand a week. That doesn't include paying the pilot."

"Charlie, you know I trust you to get the best deal possible. That's fine with me. Now, what's this idea you have?"

"We need to fly our original course through the mountains to look for the waterfall. I'll rent an Arrow, and we'll fly the same heading to Montrose. Remember I told you we passed Ohio Peak a little while before we crashed? We'll start looking there."

"And what if we don't find the waterfall?"

"We'll continue on to Montrose, stay over night, refuel, and search on the way back. We'll have plenty of fuel to cruise around south of Ohio Peak. If we fly low, I think we'll find it. When we do, I'll mark the location on my chart and note landmarks that will help us get back there. What do you think?"

"Sounds great. I like going on adventures with you. When do you plan to make the trip?"

"I'd like to go the day after tomorrow if the weather is suitable. Can you make it then?"

"Sure! What time?"

"I'll pick you up at eight in the morning. Pack an overnight case."

"I'll be ready. Can you stay for dinner?"

"I'd love to, but Sharon and I are going to a dinner show. Would you like to join us?"

"Thanks for asking, but I think not. I'm really looking forward to our search flight to Montrose. We'll have a nice dinner together there."

"Sounds good to me. Well, I'd better get going. See you at eight on Thursday. I'm looking forward to our night in Montrose too."

The wheels of the Arrow left the ground at nine o'clock. Charlie headed toward the mountains at five thousand feet. His flight chart was marked, but Charlie didn't need it. The day was clear with little wind. He flew over valleys between the peaks, adjusting their heading as necessary. He knew this flight path well.

"Leadville coming up just to our right. See it?"

Jean peered through the windscreen. "Yes, I see it. It's such a lovely clear day. Should help in finding the waterfall."

"After we pass Ohio Peak, I'll drop down, and we can start searching. Keep a lookout for that patch of light green foliage. There are lots of those patches, but hopefully, we'll find the one we crashed into. Remember, the waterfall is only a couple of miles from there."

"Yes sir, Captain."

"Hey quit that. I'm just good old Charlie. I'll let you know when I spot Ohio Peak. It's about three quarters of the way to Montrose. We're about half way now."

Jean relaxed and looked out at the rugged scenery. She was reminded of the terror when they crashed into the treetops. Thinking about Charlie's superb flying skills, she said, "Charlie, did we survive that crash landing because of your flying prowess plus a bit of luck?"

"You've got that right. We were very lucky."

Twenty minutes later Charlie saw two landmarks. "We're coming to Kebler Pass straight ahead. There's Ohio Peak on your left at about eleven o'clock. It's twelve thousand feet, and we're flying at eleven. We'll slide by the peak then drop down to about two thousand above the terrain."

"This is exciting. It's sure different from flying fast in my Saber jet at thirty thousand feet."

"Okay, we're going down now. We probably can't see the waterfall from directly over it because of the trees. I'll fly a few passes north to south, and then the reverse. You look out your side, and I'll look out mine. Maybe you'll see the mist from the falls first."

"And I'll check for spots of light green foliage too."

"We're at two thousand feet now, heading south. I'll go about ten miles then turn around and fly north. I'll move about a quarter mile over the search area each time we turn."

They made four passes in each direction and did not see the waterfall. Charlie checked the instruments. Oil pressure perfect, thank goodness.

"Two more passes in each direction and we head for Montrose. We have plenty of fuel."

Again they failed to see their elusive target. Charlie started to climb on a heading for Montrose.

"I was so sure we'd find it. I didn't even see the right patch of foliage either. Hope we have another clear day tomorrow," Jean said.

"Yeah, me too. We should see that little town where we came out of the forest in a few minutes. We're leaving some of the high mountains now."

Charlie checked the altimeter. It read five thousand feet. Smiling to himself, he climbed another two hundred feet. "We're flying at five thousand, two hundred, and eighty feet. Know what that means?" Charlie asked.

"Of course. We're a mile high."

"Right. But it also means we could join the mile-high club if this aircraft was equipped with an automatic pilot."

"What do you mean?"

"Why Jean, a woman of the world like you should know. It means…"

"Oh yes, I know, you old letch. You'd take advantage of poor little me way up here where I can't get away. Making love a mile high. I'll bet you've done that many times."

"No. Only once, many years ago."

"But Charlie, we'd have to be contortionists to make love in this little airplane."

"Not really. I'd set heading, speed, and altitude into the autopilot, and we'd climb into the backseat for fun and games."

"You sure are adventuresome, you old lecherous wolf. I'm surprised. It shows how little we know about each other. But why can't we join the club in Montrose? Surely the elevation there is above five thousand feet."

"That doesn't qualify. We have to be in an airplane at least a mile high."

"We could practice in Montrose."

"Sounds like fun to me."

That evening they soared to the clouds of ecstasy at five thousand feet.

It was mid-morning before they left the Montrose airport. Charlie climbed past five thousand feet without mentioning the mile-high club. Jean watched the altimeter as it read five thousand. Glancing at Charlie she smiled. "This mile-high is not as exciting as last night's."

Charlie smiled. "Amen!"

At eleven thousand feet they could see Ohio Peak in the distance. Charlie dropped down to two thousand feet above terrain to begin the search. As before, he flew north-south runs and the reverse, but this time extended each run to twenty miles. The river ran west to east, so the waterfall should be to either side of the airplane.

"Don't bother looking for spots of light green foliage today, Jean. Just concentrate on looking for the river or the waterfall."

"Okay," Jean replied as she peered out the side window. They had clear visibility again, but a westerly wind made it necessary for Charlie to concentrate on the instruments and controlling the airplane. He was only able to look out his side occasionally.

On the fourth southerly pass Jean shouted, "I see the river directly out to the side."

Charlie immediately turned starboard ninety degrees and saw the river in front of the airplane. "Going down for a closer look. Keep your eye on the river."

As they flew west at one thousand feet Charlie could see a mountain peak looming up in front of them about fifty miles ahead. He reduced speed to 75 knots, a little over stall speed and flew over the river for about forty miles. They did not see the waterfall. Charlie turned to the east.

"We'll fly a zigzag course crossing over the river several times, so we can look at it from the side view. Might be a better chance of spotting the waterfall that way."

"Okay. I'll keep a sharp lookout. I haven't even seen any mist or spray yet."

Flying on a southerly heading about fifty miles east of where they had turned away from the mountain peak, Jean nearly screamed. "There it is, the waterfall just off to the right."

Charlie quickly turned starboard again and lined up with the river. "I see it. I'll go as low as I can so we can get a good look."

The waterfall was barely visible through the huge trees. At one thousand feet they flew toward their pot of gold. Peering intently at the waterfall, Charlie could see the dark spot in the white spray. "That's it! I can even see the dark cave entrance behind the falls." He pulled back on the controls and climbed in an orbit around the waterfall, leveling off at ten thousand feet.

"Now we pinpoint the location. I'll mark it on my chart." After checking the chart a few seconds, Charlie marked it. "We're about 230 degrees south of Ohio Peak at about fifty miles. Now look for a closer landmark. A rock formation, a clump of tall trees, anything."

"Charlie, There's a small clearing next to the river just east of the falls."

Yes, I saw it too. Might be useful later."

They continued to circle the waterfall, looking at the surrounding terrain.

Her eyes scoured the terrain below. "I see a steep, bare cliff face to our right. Maybe about ten miles."

Charlie turned the aircraft and saw it. "That's a good landmark. It's eight to ten miles from here and northwest of our gold. I have enough locators now to find it again. Let's go home. I'll call Sharon and Tom and fill them in on our flight."

"Leave out the part about Montrose and the mile high club, please."

"You bet."

They cruised along at eleven thousand feet past Ohio Peak and Leadville. The westerly wind pushed them along nicely on their northeast route, but Charlie had to fly carefully to maintain their heading.

"Charlie, what about that clearing at the river near the falls? You said it might be useful."

"Yeah. It's too small for our chopper to land in now, but it's possible to make it bigger. We could put two woodsmen down with equipment to clear out some trees. That'd be a start of our project."

"Well, let me know how much money you'll need for that. It'll be exciting to get started. And by the way, have you found a WACO airplane yet?"

"No, not yet. We'll be back to Denver in about an hour. Tomorrow I'll start looking for my WACO."

7

THE RATHSKELLER

WHEN JAKE ARRIVED HOME FROM the airport and opened the door he heard the telephone ringing. Tossing his jacket on the kitchen table, he grabbed the phone.

"Hello. Jake here."

"Hi Jake. Tony Russo. Got a minute?"

"Just one. What's on your mind?"

"I got a call from Charlie yesterday. He said he called you about a job he needs our help with. He was pretty vague, even secretive, about what kind of job it is. I'd like to talk it over with you. How about meeting me tonight at the Rathskeller?"

"You know, Charlie's a good friend and a real nice guy. I don't know what you're worried about, but sure, I can meet you in about an hour at the Rath. My wife's got dinner ready. See ya."

Darrae, Jake's wife, came into the kitchen, picked up his jacket, and said, "I heard. Hope you're not planning on being out too late tonight talking to your buddy. Dinner's on the table. How about a glass of wine?"

"Sounds good. I'll get the Cabernet. I won't be out late. If I have to, I'll cut him off and leave. Dinner smells good. You're the best of wives, dear." Jake kissed her fondly and went to get the wine.

When Jake arrived at the Rathskeller, Tony was already sitting at the bar.

"Want a beer?" Tony urged.

"Sure."

"What the hell is Charlie up to, Jake? He said he wants to hire me in a couple of weeks for some hard work. Said it was an out-of-town job and the pay would be good. That's about all he told me, so what gives?"

Jake took a long pull on his beer and looked at Tony. "Did he also tell you to keep it to yourself not tell anyone?"

"Oh, yeah. But I figured since he called you, it would be okay for us to talk."

"Come on over to the end booth where we can't be overheard."

They slid into the booth and ordered another beer.

"Tony, having been in the service, you should know what top secret means. If not, let me refresh your memory. It means only those people with a need to know are authorized to know. That means only Charlie, you, and I have the need. Okay?"

"Sure," Tony said. "Are we getting into some secret military operation that needs civilians?"

"No," Jake replied. "But the same level of security applies. I don't know much more than you do at this point. But I do know that Charlie's been digging out information on helicopters, and I think it relates to the job. Also, I have a hunch some other people are involved. I don't know for sure, it's just that he isn't around his hangar office much lately. Of course, he doesn't have his airplane now, but still I think he's checking with other people. Twice lately he's been quick about getting off the phone when I've come into the office. That's all I know, Tony."

"Not knowing the details bothers me."

"One more thing, Tony. I've worked with Charlie for a long time and know him real well. You can be sure he'd never get involved in anything underhanded or illegal. It just isn't his style. He's as honest as the day is long. And don't worry, when the time's right, Charlie will fill us in. I've got to get on home. See ya later." Jake slid out of the booth and paused. "Remember, Tony, no one else, not even your wife."

"I know. I can keep my trap shut. See you."

Tony went to the bar and ordered another beer. His mind whirled with questions What the hell was this operation about? When's Charlie going to give us the info? Who else is in it? And hell, why the choppers? "Damn it," he said to his beer mug. "I'll be on edge thinking about this stuff until Charlie calls again." He slid off the bar stool and headed home.

Jake arrived home at a reasonable hour. His wife was crocheting and watching television. Without missing a stitch or looking at Jake she asked, "What did Tony want?"

Jake had already prepared his answer. "You know Tony. He's a klutz when it comes to fixing his car. Besides wanting to quaff a few beers, he wanted to know how to fix his carburetor. So I told him, and I only had two beers."

Jake stared at the television, but his mind didn't see the image on the screen. His thoughts were on Charlie and the job. Charlie wasn't usually secretive, he told himself. This job, this operation, must be very special. Could it have to do with the crash of his airplane? He didn't seem to care much about what the FAA would find at the crash site. But the Arrow was his pride and joy. True, it was a total loss. Why did he seem so casual, so disinterested in losing it? Hope he enlightens us on the mystery soon. Well, like I told Tony, he'll let us know when the time is right.

"Let's go to bed, Darrae," he said. "I'm tired."

"You go ahead. I've got a few more rows to crochet. Night, sweetheart."

THE BOOTH HAS EARS

Jake met Tony again at the Rathskeller. There was only one empty booth. Jake was hesitant about sitting there and as they slid onto the benches he cautioned, "Keep the talk low volume."

Tony ordered a straight-up Manhattan and Jake his usual Heineken beer. The waitress eyed Tony carefully and smiled fetchingly. "How about another Manhattan so you won't have to wait for me to come back?"

"Baby, I'd wait for you all evening. What time do you get off?"

"Eleven, but I'm booked tonight."

"We'll talk later. See ya," He smiled and twirled one end of his handlebar mustache.

"She's got the hots for you. Must be that mustache," Jake observed.

"Hope so. What's new with Charlie?"

"He's having, what he calls, a final briefing next week. We go to work on his project soon. I'm to fill you in after the meeting."

"Has he given you any more information about the job?"

"Not much. But he says he'll need us for a couple of weeks, including weekends, when you can get away from your job. It involves cutting down big trees and flying to the job site in a helicopter."

"What about the pay?"

"He says you'll get double what you'd expect for this kind of work and maybe a bonus."

"Sounds good. But Jake, you must have some idea of what this is all about. I know you're close to him. Come on, I don t want to go on a wild goose chase. Give."

"Evidently he's got some big financial backing for this."

One of the three men in the booth behind Tony signed to his buddies to be quiet. Placing a finger to his lips and pointing behind him with his other hand, he turned his head and listened intently.

Jake continued in a quiet, subdued voice. "I think he's going to build a cabin in the forest. We have to fell timber to make room for the cabin and prepare a place for the helicopter to land. I heard him mention a waterfall in one of his phone conversations. So, I presume there's a river."

Tony interjected, "Why would anyone build a camp in a place so isolated it's only accessible by helicopter? And why spend so much money?"

"Good questions, Tony. There must be more to it than Charlie's telling us. Oh, another thing, one day when I walked into his office he quickly put his hand over some thing on his desk. I got only a brief glance, but it looked like a little rock or a nugget."

"A nugget of go..."

"Stop. No more. Quiet," Jake said with a silencing gesture at Tony.

In the booth behind Jake and Tony, the listener leaned forward and whispered. "Joey, you and I leave now and see where these guys go. Murph, you stay here and pump the blond bombshell for names and any other information you can get. No rough stuff. We'll see you later. Come on, Joey."

"Don't get excited," Jake continued. "Remember, I may be wrong. It's really just a guess. Don't forget, not a word to anyone. I'll let you know when I get the final briefing. Come on. Let's go home."

In the parking lot the listeners, Mike and Joey, waited in their pickup truck. "Damn! They both have a car. We'll follow the guy with the mustache and see where he lives," Mike said.

"What did you hear that was so interesting?" Joey asked.

"I could only hear bits of it, but they have a job that's backed by big money. And it may have something to do with gold."

"Gold! Man, we may be onto something."

"Yeah, but we need more info. Maybe Murph'll get it."

After following Tony home, Mike and Joey drove quickly back to the Rathskeller. They motioned Murph sitting at the bar to join them in a booth.

"Where's the blonde bombshell?" Mike asked.

"She left five minutes ago. But I got to talk to her."

"So what'd you get?"

"A date for Saturday night," Murph smirked.

Mike rapped Murph solidly on the arm. "I don't give a damn about your date. You know what I mean."

"Okay, okay. She knew a little. The big guy works out at the airport. She thinks he's an aircraft mechanic."

"What's his name?"

"Jake. She didn't know his last name, but the bartender told me it's Burnham. The other guy with the mustache is Tony. She doesn't know anything else about him."

"Good," Mike said. "I'll take it from here. I'll check out this Jake Burnham. You may have got just enough, Murph. Come on. Let's go."

8

SHARON'S ADVICE

CHARLIE SETTLED HEAVILY INTO HIS RECLINER with a cup of coffee on the table beside him. Sharon sat on the sofa leafing through a fashion magazine.

"Sharon, can I interrupt you for a few minutes? I need your thoughts on a subject dear to my heart."

"Of course, Dad. I'm just browsing through this magazine."

"Thanks. To get right to the point, what do you think of my accepting Jean's offer to buy me an airplane? I feel kind of hesitant about it."

"Dad, right to the point as you say, I think you should accept with no misgivings at all. You know she can easily afford it and wants to show you how much she likes you. I've noticed those sly looks you give each other. Is something serious going on?"

"Oh my, aren't you the shrewd, perceptive daughter who takes after her mother. Maybe something is happening. I think she's a wonderful lady." Quickly changing the subject, "I have a friend in Kansas who owns a WACO, the model I'd like to have. He's getting on in years, and I'm hoping he might consider selling it. I'm going to give him a call right now. Thanks, my princess, for your welcomed advice."

"No thanks needed, Dad. Now let's talk more about Jean."

Charlie ignored Sharon's remark and marched into the den.

"Harry, this is Charlie out in Denver. How are you, old buddy?"

"Charlie, you old fly by the seat of your pants pilot. I'm doin' okay. You still greasing in your plane with no tire squeal? Been a long time since we've talked."

"Yeah, long time. I nearly bought the farm in my Arrow a few weeks back. It's a total wreck, but I'm okay. You still flyin' your WACO?"

"Well, just locally. No long trips anymore. I stay home with my wife. She's not too well these days."

"Sorry to hear that, Harry. I'm looking for another plane and wondered if you might consider selling your WACO? I'd love to have that plane."

"You know, Charlie, I've been thinking about selling it lately. I can't use it very often these days. I know you'd take care of it, and I'd rather sell it to you than any one else. It's up to date on inspections and still flies beautifully. I'd like to get sixty-five thousand for it. How does that strike you?"

"Sounds like a fair price to me. I know you've kept it in good shape. Would it be okay if I come to your house a week from today? I'll bring a certified check, and after we get all the paper work done, I'd like to fly the plane back here."

"Okay, and you stay the night at my house. We've got old times to talk about."

"Thanks. See you then. Goodbye."

Charlie burst out of the den, and like a kid with a new toy, announced, "I've got my WACO! I'll pick it up in a week. How about that?"

"Wonderful, Dad."

"You'll love riding in an open cockpit airplane. You know the original WACO dates back to the twenties. The plane I'm buying is a reproduction, built I think, in 1990. I'll teach you how to fly it. But now we need to talk business. We're almost ready to start our gold project. I've got a helicopter lined up, a pilot, and two men who'll cut timber. I'm calling a meeting for Saturday evening here. Will you be available?"

"Yes. I don't have any plans."

"Okay. Eight o'clock. I'll call Jean and see if she can be here. She can call Tom."

JEAN'S SECRET

Jean's housekeeper saw the letter carrier bypass the mailbox and come toward the front door. She opened the door as he reached the porch. Along with the junk mail, he handed Lydia a large certified mail envelope. She signed for it and took it quickly to Jean out on the patio.

Sipping her margarita, Jean put down her book and thanked Lydia for bringing the mail. The certified envelopc, as she expected was from a friend who was a computer "whiz." Jean had never succumbed to the lure of bytes, modems, and computer paraphernalia. Her friend found what Jean wanted on the Internet.

She opened the envelope and removed six pages of computer-generated data on the WACO aircraft. "Wonderful," she whispered to herself. She could begin her secret plan. She browsed quickly through the text and pictures, and then started to memorize the facts. She was determined to know almost as much as Charlie about a WACO.

On the commercial flight to Kansas City, Charlie reviewed the meeting of the gold claimers. Tom was laid up with walking pneumonia and couldn't be there. Jean would brief him.

The helicopter and a small front-end loader would be at Maher two weeks from today. Chain saws, axes, two small tents, food, water, and other necessary supplies would be ready to load. Charlie, Jake, and Tony would fly to Maher to meet the helicopter pilot in thirteen days. Jake and Tony had managed to get a week off from their jobs.

The chopper pilot, a friend of Charlie's, told him he'd need one crewman to operate the winch that would place the men and gear on the ground as the chopper hovered over the small clearing. Then they could clear a place big enough for the helicopter to set down.

Jean had sent the required payment to the pilot. Charlie had arranged to have supplies staged in a vacant hangar at Maher. He planned to work the men from dawn to dusk so they'd be too tired to look around the site. He figured it would take three days of hard labor to get the clearing ready for the helicopter to land.

Charlie had cautioned Jean and Sharon not to get their hopes up too high about the amount of gold ore in the cave. "There's no telling how deep or how extensive the vein is. And remember, some of it has been chipped away already. The pile of rocks in the cave, dug years ago, may be most of the vein."

Mike looked for the name in the phone book. There were three Jacob Burnhams. He hit pay dirt on the second call. When he asked, "Is you husband an airplane mechanic?"

"Yes," was the reply.

"Could you tell me what airline he works for," Mike queried.

Jake's wife answered, "Oh, he doesn't work for an airline. He only works on light aircraft. You know, single and twin engine private planes. If you leave your number, I'll have him call you."

"That's okay. I'll contact him at the airport." Mike hung up.

CHARLIE'S FIRST WACO FLIGHT

His walk around inspection ended at the tail wheel. True to his usual routine, Charlie kicked the ground. It reminded him of his Piper Arrow. Now my queen of the sky is this beautiful WACO, Charlie thought.

He slid down into the cockpit. He fit perfectly as if it was designed just for him. Familiarizing himself with the controls and the instruments, he realized they were not much different from similar aircraft he had flown.

Charlie looked at the sky. Cumulus clouds were building in the northwest as the forecast had promised. The sky south of those clouds was clear. He was departing from the little airfield at Olathe, Kansas where Harry kept his plane. Planning to fly home south of the cloud buildup, he turned onto the active runway and lined up for take-off. He glanced again at the western sky and noted its appearance hadn't changed.

As the wheels left the runway Charlie felt exhilaration rivaling the feeling he had when he first soloed years ago. The little WACO responded smoothly to his touch. He turned to a heading of 260 degrees aiming for Garden City, his alternate airport if needed. He leveled off at ten thousand feet and looked anxiously at the mass of clouds to the northwest. The sky was not a pleasant sight. Some of the dark clouds were developing classic anvil-shaped tops, the kind of formation pilots of small planes are careful to avoid. Lightning began piercing the clouds. Charlie noticed the ominous clouds slowly moving south as they dropped curtains of rain.

"Damn," he said to himself, "I'd better get to Garden City soon. Doesn't look good." He advanced the throttle to a little more than normal cruise speed. He could see the town of McPherson and route 81 directly ahead. It was the halfway point en route to Garden City. The dark, menacing clouds were getting lower and coming closer. Charlie started a slow descent to further increase speed. He was sure that soon he'd have to fly even lower to get under the heavy cumulus clouds.

Thirty minutes later he was down to two thousand feet, just under the intimidating clouds. There was no rain, only gloom. Charlie peered intently straight ahead. Garden City should be at twelve o'clock soon. Please, he thought, hold off rain. Just for a few more minutes.

A gust of wind flipped the WACO up on the left wings. Charlie fought to level the plane and descended to one thousand feet. The wind was steady now and getting stronger. Turning to stay on course, he headed into the wind and still Garden City was not in sight.

It was three o'clock in the afternoon, but it looked like dusk. The black clouds completely obscured the sun and visibility was down to about a half mile. Staring through the windscreen, Charlie saw a town and a nearby runway Garden City at last. The lowering clouds were upon him now, and he descended to five hundred feet. There was no time for a standard landing pattern. He'd go straight for the runway.

As he flew over the end of the runway at twenty feet a few drops of rain splattered on the windscreen. The WACO touched down in a perfect three-point landing just as the rain intensified. Lightning was streaking through the clouds accompanied by incessant claps of thunder. Charlie knew a deluge was imminent. He turned off the runway and taxied to a parking area near the terminal. Stopping between two tiedowns, he shut off the engine, grabbed the cockpit tarp, and hoisted himself out of the plane. He quickly covered the open cockpit and jumped down to the ground from the wing just as the clouds opened up with a torrent of rain. He attached the tiedown lines from the ground to the wings and ran toward the terminal.

By the time he reached the door, Charlie was drenched. After checking in with the operations office he gulped down a cup of coffee, found the public telephone, and called his daughter. "Hi Sharon. I'm calling from Garden City, Kansas. Some stormy weather forced me to land here. I'll stay overnight and take off in the morning. Should be at the airport by ten o'clock tomorrow morning. Call Jean and tell her. Love you, princess."

CHARLIE'S ANGEL

Sharon and Jean were at the airport at nine forty-five in the morning. Waiting in front of Charlie's hangar, they scanned the eastern sky for a two-wing airplane. The sky was clear and they could see for miles.

Jean saw a speck in the sky. "Maybe that's him," she said to Sharon pointing at the tiny dot in the blue. As it came closer they saw it was a low wing monoplane. "Come on, Charlie. We're waiting for you," Jean said anxiously.

Sharon pointed out another speck southeast of the airport. They followed its approach and soon began to hear the drone of its engine. "It's a biplane. Must be Dad," Sharon said excitedly.

"It's a WACO. I can tell from pictures I've seen. That bright red color, it's beautiful," Jean said.

Charlie touched down smoothly, taxied toward his hangar, and saw his two ladies waving at him. It was good to be back home. He turned off the engine and removed his helmet as the women came running to the airplane.

"Charlie, welcome back. Your WACO is gorgeous!" Jean said.

"Dad, we're so glad to see you. So you had some rough flying weather," Sharon said.

"Yes. I had to lay over in Garden City because of thunderstorms. It's great to be home. Well, how do you like my new airplane?"

The ladies replied in unison, "It's super!"

Jake came out of the hangar. "Man, that's a beauty, Charlie. I'll have fun working on it."

"Roll it into the hangar, Jake, and take a good look at it. She rolls easily. I've already closed out my flight plan with the tower, so come on, ladies, into my office. I'll tell you all about my new prize.

Charlie settled into his desk chair as Sharon and Jean sat facing him on the sofa. "Now let me tell you about my WACO. It's…"

"Just a minute, Charlie," Jean interrupted. "If your plane is the model I think it is, it's a taper wing WACO, and I already know a lot about it. If it has a 300 horsepower engine and a sixty-five gallon fuel tank. It can fly for about three and a half hours and go 527 miles. It…"

"Jean, hold it. What is this? How do you know all this?"

"In a minute, Charlie. It has a wingspan of 30.3 feet. The wings taper from the trailing and leading edges toward the tips. And it has a stall speed of fifty miles per hour."

Charlie and Sharon sat there dumbfounded.

Jean continued, "I can also tell you some of the history of the WACO. And if you know when this replica was built, I can tell you even more." She sat back with a smug, satisfied smile.

"Jean, you amaze me. You're a fount of information about the WACO. My replica was built in 1991. Go on."

"Your plane was probably produced as a kit by The WACO Aircraft Company in Forks, Washington. Then assembled by the owner or someone else. The cost of an assembled kit is about $70,000 or more, depending on equipment. Now, I have to refer to my notes. I couldn't memorize it all. Clayton Bruckner and Elwood "Sam" Junkin started the original WACO Aircraft Company in Ohio in the early 20s. They brought in a well-known local barnstormer, Buck Weaver, as a partner and used his name to draw interest in their product. And that's how the airplane got its name, WACO for Weaver Airplane Company. Their first plane was build in 1923. The first taperwing was produced in 1928 and won a trophy race. And that concludes my discourse on the WACO."

"Okay, now that you've impressed us with your knowledge, how did you come by all this information?" Charlie asked.

"Simple. I have a friend who's a computer whiz, so I asked her to look WACO up on the Internet. I wanted to bone-up, so to speak, on your new airplane. After all, I have a vested interest in it."

"Jean, you guessed right on the engine specs. It is three hundred horsepower, and the plane was built from a kit. How about a ride in it tomorrow?"

"I'm ready. I'll bring a bottle of champagne for the christening. By the way, what are you going to name your WACO?"

"Charlie's Angel. How's that?"

"Hmm. Reminiscent of an old TV show, but it fits nicely. I like it," Sharon said.

"Yes," Jean said, "that's a good name. This WACO is your angel."

TROUBLE BREWING

Mike drove out to the airport and turned to the general aviation side of the runways. He had planned his course of action. A good source of information about Jake could be the coffee shop. He entered slowly, looking around. Six men occupied a table near the counter. He slid onto a stool at the counter and ordered coffee and a Danish. His seat was close enough to the table so he could listen to their conversation.

As he slowly sipped his coffee, Mike could easily hear the conversation around him. But after fifteen minutes, he hadn't heard any mention of Jake. He decided to wait another fifteen minutes before going to the next phase of his inquiry. He ordered a refill of coffee.

The time passed, but still no useful information. He turned on his stool to face the men and said, “Pardon me, gentlemen, do any of you know Jake Burnham?”

One of the men spoke immediately. “Sure. Everybody knows old Jake. Why?”

“I need to find a good airplane mechanic for my boss. He just bought a Beechcraft. Jake was recommended. Where can I find him?”

“Well, Jake’s usually here for coffee with us. He must be workin’ on one of his planes down in hangar eight. He’s a busy guy.”

“Thanks, I’ll go see if I can find him.”

Mike walked down the flight line toward hangar eight. He mentally reviewed what he’d say to Jake. The big hangar doors were open allowing Mike to see three airplanes housed there. He also saw a man working on one of the planes and ambled slowly toward him. “I’m looking for Jake Burnham. Is that you?”

“No, Jake’s there at the back of the hangar.”

“Thanks.”

Mike saw a man at the workbench. He walked quickly to him. “Hi, if you’re Jake Burnham, I’d like to talk with you for a minute.”

“Sure, but I have to keep working on this carburetor,” Jake said, turning to look at Mike before going back to his work. “Go ahead.”

“My name’s Harry Jones. My boss just bought a Cessna and told me to find a mechanic to maintain it. You were recommended.”

“Oh. What kind of Cessna? There are several models.”

“I don’t know. I haven’t seen it.”

“Well, I’ve got all I can handle with four planes now. I couldn’t take on another one. Sorry.”

“That’s okay. But my boss is going to be disappointed. Say, do you ever fly with your airplane owners?”

“Sometimes we go up together.”

“My boss flies to some place in the mountains to get away and relax. Do any of your pilots fly to the mountains?”

“Sometimes. Why?”

“Oh, just curious. Do you ever go to a camp or some place up there?”

Jake continued his work, thinking, what's this guy really got on his mind? Sounds like he's fishing. He turned to say, "Look Harry, I'm busy and need to concentrate on this carburetor. You better go find yourself another mechanic."

"Geez, you don't have to be so up-tight."

Jake ignored him so Mike turned and walked out of the hangar.

As Jake continued working, he said to himself, "I'd better tell Charlie about this."

9

TO THE WILDERNESS AGAIN

CHARLIE RENTED A CESSNA FOR THE FLIGHT to Montrose. While doing the preflight walk-around inspection, he cautioned Jake, "Don't tell Tony anything except our destination. I'll fill him in on the job. Oh, by the way, thanks for telling me about your encounter in the hangar." Tony came out of the coffee shop as they finished the inspection.

They flew the same route Charlie had flown in the Arrow. Flying past Ohio Peak, Charlie looked down at the wilderness and thought maybe they were crazy trying to get that gold. He checked the gauges, especially noting the oil pressure. No problem. Jake and Tony were silent most of the trip.

As they descended at Montrose, Charlie saw the helicopter waiting in front of the old hangar. "Okay, you guys. This is Montrose, and there's our chopper right on schedule." He parked next to the big Boeing Vertol. The pilot wasn't there.

Tony exclaimed, "Man, that's a big chopper. I've never seen one like this."

"It's what we need to do the job," Charlie advised. "Let's go over to the Ops Office. I have to close out my flight plan. Maybe Chet, the chopper pilot, is there."

Charlie closed his flight plan and checked the weather forecast. It looked good for tomorrow's flight. Jake and Tony had gone into the adjoining coffee shop. As Charlie entered he spotted Chet and another man seated at a table. Striding over to them, he called out, "Chet, you old hovering pilot. Good to see you again. Been a long time."

"Charlie, how's it goin'? Looks like you got out of your Arrow crash in one piece."

"Yeah, but you should see what's left of the plane. You been waitin' here long?"

"We've been here since about ten this morning. Charlie, meet Tommy. He's my winch operator."

The two men nodded and shook hands as Jake and Tony came over to the table. Introductions were made, and they all sat down. A waitress came to take their orders.

"Chet, I checked the weather. It looks fine for tomorrow. Let's load the chopper now so we can be ready to go early."

"Hey, what do you think Tommy and I've been doing loafin' in the sun? We've got everything loaded already, including the small generator, forklift, and front-end loader you called me about. Everything is all tied down and ready to go. Let's go get a motel. I'd like to lift off at eight in the morning."

"Thanks, guys. You sure saved us a lot of work. Let's put the chopper in the hangar and tie down the Cessna outside. I'm planning to sleep in the hangar tonight just to make sure nobody messes with our stuff. I've got a bedroll in the Cessna. Turning to Jake and Tony, Charlie continued, "You guys get a good night's sleep. Tomorrow we start clearing for my client's lodge."

Later, as he unrolled the bedroll, Charlie thought again about something that was troubling him. A couple of days ago, when he was sitting with the mechanics in the coffee shop at the terminal in Denver, one of them told him about a man who came in wanting to hire an airplane mechanic for a Beechcraft. The guy was about six feet tall and hefty, dressed in jeans, plaid shirt, and cowboy boots. It sounded like the same one who talked to Jake about hiring him for a Cessna. When Jake described the encounter to him, it sounded phony. Charlie suspected something, but what? Not taking any chances, he placed his thirty-eight pistol beside him in the bedroll.

BACK TO THE WATERFALL

After an uneventful night in the hangar Charlie gathered his crew together before pushing the helicopter out on the tarmac. "Here's how we operate on this job. I'll sit up front with Chet so I can navigate to our place in the forest. Chet, start out on a heading of 070 degrees at ten thousand feet. Go lower when we're close so I can see my landmarks. When we get to our destination, hover as low as possible over the small clearing."

Chet interrupted, "How low do you think I'll be able to take it?"

"Low enough so your winch cable can lower the equipment and us to the ground. I don't think you'll have a wind problem so holding the chopper steady shouldn't be difficult. Jake, Tony, and I will go down first. Chet, can the two of you manage to get our stuff out and down to us?"

"Tommy can do it himself while I hold the chopper steady. The heavy stuff is on slide tracks so he can line it up at the door. And we have a sling for you guys to go down in."

"Okay. When everything is unloaded you guys fly back to Montrose. Here's enough money for your expenses. I figure we can clear a big enough area for you to land on in three days. Come back to pick us up Friday at about two in the afternoon."

"Now, as to why we are doing this thing, this job. Our employer is a wealthy woman who wants a secluded, private place where she can relax and get away from it all. We happened upon this spot when we walked away from the crash of my Arrow, and she fell in love with it. After we clear a place for the chopper to land she'll come to look things over and decide about building her lodge."

"I plan for the three of us to clear land from dawn to dusk. We'll be too tired to explore and enjoy the scenery. Any questions?"

"Yeah," Tony spoke quickly. "When do I get paid?"

"As soon as we get back to Denver. And you get a handsome bonus if we complete the job on time. Is that okay?"

"Okay."

"Let's go," Charlie urged. "Let's get the chopper out of the hangar."

They lifted off at 9:20 in the morning and Chet turned to the 070 heading. Twenty miles later they flew over Maher, the little town the crash survivors had seen when they emerged from the wilderness. Soon they were over the Gunnison National Forest and Charlie looked for the 12,250-foot Ohio Peak. The day was clear and visibility was excellent, he'd spot it easily.

Fifty minutes into the flight Charlie saw the peak off to their right. "Chet, in about ten miles I want you to circle right and orbit about a twenty mile circle. We're close to the place."

In a few minutes Charlie advised, "Start your circle now." As he looked forward and to the starboard. "Go down to seven thousand feet, Chet. I need a closer look." After ten minutes Charlie instructed, "Go 070 for three minutes and descend to five thousand feet." Charlie's head swiveled back and forth looking for his two landmarks. At the lower altitude Charlie said, "Now, a fifteen mile circle at four thousand feet."

Charlie saw the rock-faced cliff near the river five minutes later. "Go down to two thousand feet and tighten it up, make a smaller pattern." The helicopter descended, and there it was the waterfall, the river, and the clearing. "Okay, Chet. At two o'clock, see the river and the waterfall?"

"Yeah, I got it."

"Down river from the waterfall about three hundred yards, see the small clearing?"

"Yeah, I see it."

"That's where we unload and you leave us. Take it down slowly. How's the wind?"

"Minimal. No problem. We'll be steady in about three minutes."

Charlie went back to get into the sling. He was ready when Chet started the nearly motionless hover. Tommy pushed Charlie out on the winch arm and started the winch mechanism. Halfway down, the sling jerked to a stop. Charlie hung there swaying fifty feet above the ground. Looking up at the chopper, he heard Tommy curse, "Damn." Tommy adjusted the cable and the winch started with a jerk, lowering Charlie the remaining fifty feet. The other two woodsmen followed. Chet moved the helicopter slightly and down came the small forklift and generator. All of their equipment and supplies were on the ground in thirty minutes. Charlie signaled Chet to depart, and the chopper slowly lifted and flew out of sight.

"First we put up our tent, over here out of the way," Charlie pointed, "and put our food, water, and bedrolls in it. Then we'll gas up the chain saws and clear the small trees and brush out of the clearing. Take your cuttings about fifty feet into the woods on the east and west sides. After that we'll move the generator and the forklift to the north side of the clearing. Tomorrow we'll start on the big trees there."

"I'll lay a fire for our dinner and get stuff organized in the tent while you guys start clearing. We'll work until dark, and then have dinner and a good sleep in this fresh air. How does that sound?"

"Okay, you slave driver," Jake laughed.

"Right on," Tony said grudgingly.

To the west, a mountain peak seemed to pierce the bright yellow sun. Clouds, tinted with streaks of pink, copper-red, and ocher-orange hovered above the mountains. Charlie felt the air cool as he looked up from his bundle of kindling. He had to stop and marvel at the beautiful panorama of shifting colors. This scene could never be captured in a painting. The colors on the palette in the sky became even more beautiful as the sun began to set.

"I'll start the fire now, guys. We'll have ham, fried potatoes, green beans, bread, and coffee. For dessert, an apple," Charlie shouted over the sound of chainsaws.

Dusk came and would be quickly followed by total darkness here in the valley. "Go down to the river and clean up, guys. Dinner's almost ready." Charlie knew the dusk and creeping darkness would obscure any flashes of gold from nuggets in the river.

Jake and Tony complimented Charlie on his hearty dinner as they sipped their strong, steaming coffee. Tony asked, "How'd you become such a good outdoorsman and cook? That was great chow."

"Okay, before we get too sleepy, I'll tell you a story," Charlie answered.

"Ah, a bedtime story." Jake chuckled.

"Not exactly. I spent time hiking and hunting in Alaska with one other guy. We spent two weeks in Mount McKinley National Park and the surrounding forest hunting grizzlies and other bears. We learned to travel light and cook over campfires. What fantastic sights we saw! Mount McKinley is over 20,900 feet, making it the highest in North America. It was an awe-inspiring sight. We saw glaciers and a beaver dam that was at least one hundred feet long. The time to go on a trip like that is between June and September. Winter's not the time. I was up there with the Air Force in winter and experienced a couple days of minus sixty-three degrees. But that's another story."

"Tomorrow's bedtime story?" Jake smiled.

Charlie grinned and continued. "One more thing about being a woodsman. When you're in the wilderness, you have to put your food in a place where animals can't get to it. Up there in Alaska, we built a solidly enclosed tree hut for food or hung it from a high branch. Since we're here for only a few days, I'm keeping our food in that airtight locker we brought. It should keep the smell of food from bears."

"Oh no! Are there bears around here?" Tony asked.

"Probably. Mountain lions too." Charlie decided not to tell them about his encounter with a mountain lion. "I have a thirty-eight revolver in case it's ever needed. Well, let's clean up our mess here and get some sleep. Oh, one more thing, I dug a latrine for us out by the brush piles. See you bright and early tomorrow."

Before going to sleep, Charlie pondered the problem of how to keep Jake and Tony away from the river during the day when the glitter of gold might be seen. He fell asleep before finding a solution.

THE NEXT DAY

As if he were an automaton, Charlie's eyes opened right on schedule the first light of dawn. The second thing he saw, after the tent roof, was the pail of water near the tent flap. Along with the dawn of day, the dawn of an idea popped into his brain. At lunchtime his crew could wash up at the pail instead of at the river. Also, he remembered the trees on both sides of the river formed an umbrella of shade over the water. A short break in early morning or late afternoon would be enough time to satisfy any curiosity about the river. He would have to make sure to be with them to explain away any sparkle in the water.

After scrambled eggs, ham, and coffee, they went to work. The small clearing was now devoid of brush and small trees.

“We’ll start on the north side,” Charlie advised, “by felling the trees into this clearing, stripping the branches, and cutting them into about six foot lengths. We’ll forklift the logs to the sides near our other cuttings. I figure we need to cut back to the north about forty feet. Then we start widening the east and west sides. The south cut will be about twenty feet. Our finished clearing has to be about one hundred feet square. The helicopter can set down in that space.”

“Where do you want the generator and the forklift?” Jake asked.

“Over in the southeast corner of the clearing.”

“I’ll move ‘em.”

“Good. Come on, Tony. We’ll start on the north forty.”

By lunchtime they had cut and cleared twenty feet of the north border. They cleaned up at the water bucket, made sandwiches, drank beer, and rested their aching muscles. There was no mention of going to the river, which pleased Charlie.

About four in the afternoon Charlie said, “Let’s take a half hour break. We’re making good progress.”

“I’m all for that,” Jake agreed.

“Yeah! Me too,” Tony huffed as he put down the chain saw.

“Let’s go down to the river and cool off,” Jake suggested.

“Okay, “ Charlie said, “but just splash some water on yourselves. Don’t go wading. And watch for bear tracks by the water.” That’ll give them something to think about Charlie mused as he looked at the sky. Gray clouds were hiding the sun. Mother nature was cooperating.

“Hey, Charlie. Come here,” Jake exclaimed as he kneeled down near the river. “Is this what I think it is?”

Charlie knelt down beside Jake. “If you think that’s a bear track, you’re right on the money.”

"Damn."

After about fifteen minutes Charlie ordered, "Come on, guys. Back to work." Thankful there had been no mention of anything sparkling in the water.

Muttering humorously about shortened work breaks and slave conditions, they reluctantly returned to the job.

Dusk was upon them, and all three were glad to see it. They needed a rest. The north forty was cleared.

"Hey, boss. How about cooling off and cleaning up in the river?" Tony asked.

"Good idea," Charlie agreed. "Then we build a fire and have chow. Who wants to peel potatoes? I'll fix the rest."

They were in their bedrolls early. Charlie put his revolver beside him. All three were asleep by nine o'clock. Scudding clouds intermittently covered the half moon and stars. The quiet of the night was intensified by the vastness of the forest darkness.

Some time during the night, Charlie's keen hearing made him aware of a strange sound. He woke up immediately alert and reached for his thirty-eight. He lay still, listening. There was a soft shuffling or scratching sound coming from something near the tent. Tony and Jake were still sound asleep. Charlie slowly pulled the revolver out of the bedroll. He had heard that sound before in Alaska. It was the sound of a bear rubbing himself against a tree. He heard what sounded like the grunt of the bear. Lie still. Wait. It must be a bear. It might go away after its curiosity is satisfied. The wait seemed endless. The creature padded along softly toward the front of the tent. Charlie aimed at the tent flap, which was tied closed. *Please guys, no sound*, Charlie thought, *stay asleep*.

The shuffling sound of bear paws seemed to move away from the tent. Then the sound stopped. Gun in hand, Charlie slowly slid from his bedroll. He eased over to the tent flap and pulled the flap back just enough to see out. The bear was sniffing and pawing the cold remnants of the cook fire. He must smell leavings from our dinner. We'll have to be a lot more careful, he cautioned himself.

The bear gave up on foraging and after staring at the tent a moment, he waddled off to the edge of the clearing and disappeared into the forest. Charlie sighed with relief but untied the flap and cautiously stepped out of the tent. Standing motionless, he focused on the spot where the bear had disappeared. The bear could be hiding there and watching Charlie. After watching for several minutes and making sure there was no sound or movement of bushes, Charlie slipped back into the tent, slid into his bedroll, and fell asleep immediately.

The next day at breakfast Charlie asked, "Did you guys hear a prowler last night?"

Jake and Tony looked at him in silent apprehension.

"We had a bear check us out last night." He nosed around the cook fire. Must have smelled something left over from dinner. We'll have to be more careful about that."

"Jeez, I'm glad I didn't see him. This is the first time I've been glad you work us so hard. I think I died when I hit the sack," Jake answered.

"Yeah, me too," Tony agreed.

They worked on the east twenty that day. Charlie didn't drive them so hard. He knew they were ahead of schedule. They finished clearing on the east side at four in the afternoon.

After taking the last of the cuttings into the woods, Charlie rasped through a cough, "Good day's work, guys. Let's knock-off now and cool off in the river." Clouds moving slowly overhead were keeping the sun from shining too brightly on the water. The nuggets shouldn't be evident. To be on the safe side, he'd take them up to the falls where they could soak themselves in the pool at the base of the waterfall. The swirling, churning water would obscure any glint of gold. And if they noticed the dark shadow in the middle of the cascading water, he was sure they wouldn't realize its significance. All three of the men swam and cavorted in the pool. Jake and Tony enjoyed the cool bath so much they had no curiosity about their surroundings.

Jake remarked, "What a beautiful waterfall. This is a perfect place to commune with nature and get away from it all."

"Sure is," Charlie confirmed as he glanced at the curtain of water.

"Our employer, with her money, can turn this place into a beautiful haven of peace and solitude."

"Where did she get all her bucks, Charlie?" Tony inquired.

"She's a widow, married millionaires twice. They both left her most of their money."

"Man, lucky lady, two times."

"Let's go, men. I'm hungry. I'll make us hamburgers and potatoes for dinner. Then we can sit around the fire, tell war stories, and watch for bears."

"Hey, I'm a city boy. No bears for me," Tony implored.

"Keep that thirty-eight handy tonight, Charlie," Jake muttered. "I'm glad you're a light sleeper."

"Don't worry. I'll be ready, but I don't think that bear will come around again as long as we're careful about cleaning up after we eat."

THE CHOPPER RETURNS

It rained that night, a slow drizzle. The ground was wet but not muddy. The bear had not visited them again, perhaps because of the rain. During breakfast Charlie outlined the schedule for the day. "We should be able to finish the south side this morning. After lunch we pack up all of the gear and be ready for the chopper pickup at two this afternoon. After we get packed we'll lay a fire with some green leaves on top for more smoke. That'll be a beacon to make it easier for Chet to find us. The weather looks good so he should be on schedule. Let's drink up, guys, and get to work."

Tony gulped his coffee and said, "I'm sure glad we're almost done. This city boy wasn't cut out to be a frontiersman."

"Same here," Jake agreed. "I'd rather get greasy working on your airplane engine any time, Charlie."

They cleared the south side easily because they had learned the tricks of the trade. Their muscles didn't protest as much now, and they moved at a faster pace. They felt lucky because nothing had broken down and no one had gotten hurt or sick. The last pile of cut logs and brush was deposited in the woods at eleven-thirty.

"You've earned a handsome bonus, guys." Charlie promised, smiling broadly. "You worked hard. Let's grab some lunch."

"Does this mean you're breaking our chains of bondage, and we're free at last," Jake joked.

"You could say that, but it only means you've done a hard job in record time and I appreciate it."

"How much is that bonus you promised?" Tony asked.

"I'm keeping that a secret for now. But you'll be pleasantly surprised. After all our employer is a very wealthy lady."

After lunch, which included river-cooled beer, they began packing their gear.

"Let's put everything in the southeast corner of the clearing and build the fire near the northwest corner, but not too close to the woods," Charlie rasped as he coughed. "Tony, get some dry tinder and small branches together and add some greenery on top. Make it twice as big as our cook fire." *Damn, hope I'm not catching a cold*, Charlie moaned to himself as he stretched his aching muscles.

Jake and Charlie finished placing the loader, generator, and supplies in the southeast corner as Tony prepared the fire. A little before two o'clock, he lit the fire, and they stretched out on the ground to relax and watch the smoke rise slowly over the trees. Two o'clock came and went.

"Damn it. Where is he?" Tony bristled.

"Have some patience, Tony," Charlie growled.

"Remind me to refuse next time you try to recruit me."

At twenty after two Charlie cocked an ear to the distant, unmistakable sound of a chopper.

"Here he comes," Charlie yelled.

"Hot damn," Tony exclaimed. "Free at last."

They all got up and looked to the sky. The big banana-shaped copter was soon hovering over them and began descending. Chet put the craft down in the middle of the clearing and shut down the engines.

As Chet came to the door Charlie waved and hollered, "Did our smoke signal help you find us?"

"Sure did. I saw it from fifteen miles away."

They loaded everything and in an hour were ready to lift off. Jake and Tony settled into their uncomfortable bench seats as Charlie slid into the co-pilot seat.

Tony inquired, "Charlie, how about staying in Montrose tonight and having a hot shower and a big, juicy steak dinner?"

"I'm way ahead of you. We have reservations at the Holiday Inn. I'm sure there'll be steak on the menu."

"Right on."

Jake interjected, "I'm for that, Charlie. Thanks."

"We'll take off for Denver tomorrow morning at ten o'clock sharp," Charlie advised.

The helicopter lifted off at four o'clock. "Charlie, you guys sure did a nice job of clearing. I had plenty of space," Chet said.

"Thanks. Head for Montrose. We need a comfortable bed for a change and a hot shower." Charlie leaned back in the co-pilot's seat and thought about what had to be done next to retrieve the gold get a smaller helicopter, stake the claim, get the gold out of the cave, and back to Denver. Too tired to plan these things, he closed his eyes and dozed off.

10

CONSPIRACY

MIKE AND HIS FELLOW CONSPIRATORS, Joey and Murph, met at the Rathskeller in an empty corner booth. A waitress, not the blonde bombshell, took their orders. Murph, in his usual smirking manner, leered at her low cut blouse as she bent over to wipe the table.

"Where's blondie? She workin' tonight?" Joey asked.

"She'll be here in about an hour, sir."

"He ain't no sir, babe. He don't have no title," Murph sneered.

"Cool it, Murph." Mike admonished as the red-haired waitress went to get their drinks. "Listen you guys, I've been doin' some gumshoe work lately and I think I've got a plan. I found out from a buddy in the control tower at Centennial that our marks flew to Montrose, Colorado. What they're doing there, I don't know."

Mike stopped talking as the waitress returned with drinks. Murph leered again, and Mike kicked him under the table.

"I don't know when they're due back. And besides Jake, the mechanic, and the pilot, Charlie, another guy was on the plane. I don't have any other contacts that can help us find out what's goin' on."

"So what's our next move?" Joey wondered.

"I think we have to bug the pilot's office in the hangar. Oh yeah, that reminds me. He just bought a new airplane, a WACO. It's in the hangar now."

"He must have a few bucks," Murph said as he took a long drag on his cigarette.

"Yeah," Mike agreed. "Murph, do you still know that electronics guy who can bug a telephone?"

"Yeah. The guy's good. It takes him about three minutes to bug a phone. That costs about two hundred clams. For three more, he'll put another bug in the room hooked up to a recorder."

"Can you guys put in a hundred and fifty each? I'll put in two hundred," Mike stated.

"I can," Joey said.

"Yeah, me too," Murph grinned.

"Okay. I'll check out the hangar office to see how we can get in. Murph, you contact your bug guy and see if he can pull off the job next Sunday night. Shouldn't be too many people around then."

The blonde bombshell strolled into the bar and spotted Joey. She was dressed in a deeply V-cut blouse and skin-tight jeans. Her four-inch heels clicked on the floor as she swayed sexily over to their table.

"Hi guys. I'm not working tonight, Joey. Let's go have some fun."

Joey stood up, put his arm around her waist, and with a wide grin said, "This is Kim, guys. We're going out and have a ball."

Murph ogled Kim and giggled, "Yeah right. Joe'll make sure you have a ball." Murph smirked and gulped down his beer.

"Let's get out of here, away from this animal," Kim said disgustedly.

"Go ahead, Joey. I'll call ya later," Mike said.

After Joey and Kim left the booth, Mike looked at Murph and thought, *Jeez, he reminds me of Richard Widmark in that movie where he shoves the old lady in a wheel chair down the stairs. That cackling giggle, that sneering look, it all fits. Hope he isn't a sadist like the guy in the flick.*

"I'm leavin' now, Murph. I'm going to check out the general aviation side of the airport to get the lay of the land, see how many people are around at night and stuff. You get a hold of your bug guy and let me know if he can do the job next Sunday. See ya later."

As Mike slid out of the booth, Murph said, "Okay. I'll call ya day after tomorrow. I'm gonna have another beer."

FUN AND GAMES

One of the first things Charlie did when they returned to Denver was to go look at his WACO. Jake was with him as they admired this replica of a barnstorming machine.

"Jake, I want to take her up for the christening flight a week from tomorrow. Check out the engine and flight controls, please, and do a complete service. I don't think you'll find any problems. The FAA inspection is current. I'm planning on taking Jean up for that flight. You might as well know now that Jean is our financial angel, and she bought me this airplane."

"Why Charlie, you sly old curmudgeon, how'd you get her to give you this fine aircraft?"

"Now, now, Jake. Don't jump to conclusions. It's true she likes me and really wanted to replace my Arrow. And this is the airplane I wanted. So, knowing she can easily afford it, I accepted her kind offer."

"Okay. No more speculation. After your ride with Jean, will it be my turn?"

"Of course, Jake. I'm going into my office now to make some phone calls."

Charlie dialed Jean's number. As the answering machine started its canned message, he slammed down the telephone. "Damn it," he grumbled, "I don't want to talk to a machine." He went into his R & R room and stretching out on the bed he mumbled to himself, "Maybe I am an old curmudgeon. Sure wish Jean was here." His thoughts turned to Operation Arrow the gold. First, I'll have to get checked-out in a chopper. I'll get Chet to check rental and lease fees on some copters for me. We'll need one big enough for four people and a heavy load. Maybe Jean would buy one. Then we have to stake our claim and file it. Next, the hard work chipping away at that vein of gold and loading ore. Damn, how the hell are we going to get heavy bags of ore out of the cave, along that twelve-inch ledge, and over to the chopper? I'll figure that out later. He got up, went to the telephone, and dialed Jean's number again.

"Hello, Jean here."

"Hi, Jean, Charlie. I was wondering if you could come over to my office. We need to make some preliminary plans for Operation Arrow."

"Yes, I could, but shouldn't all four of us meet?"

"That'll come a little later. I just want to check out some ideas I have with you before an official meeting. Okay?"

"Okay. I can be there in an hour. After our, ah, talk, let's go to dinner at one of my favorite restaurants, Le Normandy. It's a quaint little French restaurant not far from the airport"

"Sounds great. I've never been there."

"See you soon."

"Right. Bye."

He gazed out the window. The majestic mountain peaks, in their rugged beauty, pierced the sky. Scudding cumulus clouds, driven before a brisk wind, raced past the mountains as if to escape the danger of those grim peaks above the timberline where the thick carpet of trees covering the hills and lower mountains abruptly ended. It was a scene of wild beauty, Charlie mused. Teddy Roosevelt was right to attempt to describe the Rocky Mountains would bankrupt the English language.

His thoughts turned back to gold. Maybe we could build a wooden chute or trough from near the mouth of the cave over to the riverbank and slide the ore out. Then we wouldn't have to carry it along that slippery ledge. We could drag bags of ore on a path to the chopper. Wonder how deep that vein of gold is? Maybe only a half-inch, maybe twelve inches. That vein sure looks rich. Best thing to do is have some samples assayed as soon as the claim is filed before Jean spends any more money on this operation. Thinking of money, I wonder how rich Jean really is?

I better call Tom when he gets off work and bring him up to date, Charlie thought. I'll call Sharon now at her office. He dialed, but she was out on a modeling assignment.

Well, guess I'll have a little siesta before Jean gets here. He stretched out on his bed in the R & R room.

Jean entered the hangar office without knocking. The room was empty. She looked at the closed R & R room door. "He must be in there," she murmured. She opened the door silently and eased in. Charlie was sound asleep, breathing softly. Jean gazed at him, admiring his strong, lithe body. She sat gently on the edge of the bed next to him. Charlie didn't move. Leaning over, she placed her mouth next to his ear and whispered, "Shall I get undressed?" Still, Charlie remained motionless like a reposed statue.

He looks so peaceful and content. I can't wake him now. She went quietly to the other side of the bed and delicately lay down next to Charlie. She closed her eyes and fantasized about their lovemaking. In her half-conscious state she heard, "Yes." She opened her eyes and looked at Charlie. He was still motionless with eyes closed. But something was different about his face the corners of his mouth were slightly turned up. She looked at him intently. An eyelid fluttered briefly. You rascal, she thought, you heard me and faked being asleep.

She got up from the bed slowly and quietly, went to the door, and said in audible whisper, "I can't wake him. He's so peaceful. I'll come back later." She stepped into the office, silently closed the door, and turned to face it. Placing her hands on her hips, she conjured up a mean look.

She heard, "Jean, Jean, hold on, don't leave, please!" The door opened and Charlie came to an abrupt halt when he saw the expression on Jean's face.

"You rascal, you," Jean bristled. "You heard me whisper in your ear and played dead. Two can play that game."

Charlie laughed, coaxing, "Now that this game is over, how about some fun and games and etc. in the, ah, etc. room. I never really intended to talk about gold. I just wanted to see you."

"You sexy, devil, you. Come on." Unbuttoning her blouse, she led the way into the R & R and etc. room.

They left the hangar, smiling broadly, and went to their own cars. It was six o'clock and the sun was about to hide behind the mountains.

MIKE CASES THE HANGAR

Mike drove slowly, looking around for cars and people as he entered the airport. It was a dark, cloudy night, but road and parking lot lights illuminated the way. There were few cars in the main parking lot, and he didn't see any people. He turned onto the perimeter road leading to the general aviation side of the airfield. The only movement was a car traveling toward him. After it passed by he pulled into a small lot three hangars away from number eight, Charlie's hangar. He shut off the lights, leaned down below the dashboard, and lit a cigarette. Focused on number eight, he decided to wait ten minutes before getting out of the car.

Seeing no activity, Mike got out, shut the door silently, and walked toward the hangar about a quarter mile away. Halfway there he heard a car door slam and quickly ducked into the bushes beside the road. Seconds later, car lights came on near hangar eight and a car came down the road. He pushed himself further into the bushes and stood motionless. As the car passed him, Mike saw it was big, not Charlie's small MG, a Rolls Royce with a woman driving. He didn't move until the car was well out of sight. Looking around, he didn't see any activity so he continued toward the hangar.

Reaching a place between streetlights, he crossed the road and walked furtively to the hangar, waiting a few minutes, listening for any sound. Hearing nothing, he checked along the side of the building for a way in. He came to a window and just beyond it, a door. Pressing his flashlight against the windowpane, he switched it on. The room was obviously an office, apparently empty. He turned off the flashlight and tried lifting the lower half of the window, but it was locked. He went to the door and turned the knob. It, too, was locked.

Mike kneeled down and peered intently at the lock, a cheap, simple lock, not a deadbolt. He looked around to make sure no one was in sight before taking his lock-pick out of his pocket and inserting it into the keyhole. In ten seconds, the lock clicked and the door opened.

Stepping inside, he closed the door and stood still while his eyes adjusted to the darkness. Dimly visible were the desk, a telephone, a desk chair, and another chair. Mike went to the window, unlocked it, and pulled the window shade down about three inches to cover the lock. Across the room he saw a door. After a quick look out the window, he went to the inner door. Mike smiled at the sign on the door, R&R Room.

It wasn't locked and he stepped inside. A single bed, a chest of drawers, and one chair furnished the room. He thought, maybe we should have a bug put in here too.

Back in the hangar office, Mike sat at the desk and pulled the mini flashlight from his pocket. Holding the light down, shaded by his body from the window, Mike opened the center drawer and looked carefully at the contents. Nothing should be moved so that the break-in would go undetected. There were no clues about Charlie's project anywhere. He checked all the desk drawers and found nothing significant.

Mike thought it looked easy to bug the place and decided to get out of there. He looked out the window then went to the door, thumbed the lock on the inside knob, and slipped out quickly, shutting the door firmly behind him.

Staying close to the building, he edged to the corner nearest the road. Pausing to look around carefully, he walked to his car. Driving slowly out of the airport, he concluded it had been an easy casing job.

HELICOPTER TRAINING

Charlie hovered at one hundred feet over the big X painted on the ground below the helicopter. He and Chet were flying a six-passenger Eurocopter EC135 with a 356-mile range, and a 6,400-pound load capacity. Charlie had looked at Bell and Robinson copters and decided they were too small. The Eurocopter was the one for the job.

"Okay, Charlie, descend slowly and set us down right on the mark," Chet instructed.

"Piece of cake," Charlie said confidently as he began to lose altitude.

"Slow your descent, you big oaf, and touch down feather light."

Charlie did it unerringly.

"Now, we're facing 090 degrees. I want you to lift off and quickly turn to 270 degrees while climbing. Don't drag the tail. Head for the trees at the edge of the meadow and get to at least two hundred feet over the trees. Go."

Charlie did as instructed and hovered at 230 feet over the trees.

"Okay, fly boy, head back to the airport. You're doin' great. I think you're ready for your check ride and a license."

"Right on. Thanks, Chet, for getting me ready. Let's have a drink at my office when we get back."

"Okay, but a quick one. I've got to get home."

Charlie poured a Harper's bourbon for Chet and a Ballantine's scotch for himself. They sipped their drinks and relived some of the old days when they flew F-86 jets in Korea. As Chet got up to leave, the telephone rang.

"Hello, Charlie." It was his daughter, Sharon. "Just a minute, princess. Chet, our chopper pilot is just leaving." He turned to Chet. "Thanks again, Chet, See you soon."

"Hi, Sharon, what's up."

"Dad, Tom called and wanted to talk about our project in the mountains. I said no and that he should talk to you."

"Any idea what he wanted?"

"Not exactly, but I got the idea he's concerned about getting his share of the gold. Another thing, he told me that he and Jean are no longer an item, if you know what I mean."

"I know your modern idioms, princess."

"Evidently Jean sent him a 'Dear John' letter. I told him to talk to you about that too. He said he'd call you to arrange a meeting."

"Okay. I'll just wait to hear from him then."

"Dad, when do I get a ride in the WACO? And will you teach me to fly it?"

"Soon, princess, and of course I'll show you how to fly Charlie's

Angel. I'm taking Jean up Sunday for the christening flight."

"Dad, I think it bothers Tom that Jean is seeing so much of you."

"Too bad! That's his problem, not mine. Don't worry, if he brings up the subject, I know how to handle him."

"Good. When will we have our next meeting on Project Arrow?"

"As soon as I get my helicopter pilot license and that may be next week. We've got lots of planning and scheduling to do before we can get to the riches of the mountains."

"Great! Be careful with Tom. He's so unpredictable. Bye now."

"Bye, Sharon. See you soon."

Tom could be big trouble, not only in the mountains, but after they returned with the gold. He would bear close watching. I'm glad Jean dropped him. Jean, I wonder...Maybe we...His thoughts flowed to the shore of bold conjecture where he dreamed of Jean and sensual ecstasy.

TOM'S DECISION

Charlie touched down in a perfect three-point landing and taxied the WACO to his hangar. As they climbed out of the airplane, Jean's enthusiasm bubbled over. "Charlie, that was exhilarating. I love open cockpit flying. Charlie's Angel is quite noisy, but I don't care. And that loop we did was so exciting! First time for me, that stunt flying."

"Glad you enjoyed the ride. I'll do some other stunts when we go up next time."

"Your WACO is now officially christened. I'm so happy I bought it for you, Charlie."

"Your idea for the christening was very clever. Pouring a shot glass of champagne over the cowling ensured there wouldn't be any dents made by a bottle. Again, thanks for getting me this airplane." Charlie pulled her to him and kissed her.

"Mmm! Charlie, I, I, oh nothing. I know Tom is coming over. I'd better leave before he gets here. I don't want to see him. Call and let me know what he says. Okay?"

"Of course. See you. Bye."

Jean walked quickly to her car, and Charlie helped Jake push the WACO into the hangar.

In his office Charlie opened the tech manual that his friend in Kansas had given him. If I'm going to be a tail-dragger pilot, he mused, I better bone up on this aircraft. Tail-dragger, that's what the pilots were called in the old days. Some of the old planes had only a tail-skid to keep the tail off the ground before progressing to a wheel. He had just started to read about tapered wings and wing struts when the door opened suddenly and Tom walked in.

"Tom, I expected a knock before you charged in."

"Sorry, I..."

"Never mind. Sit down. What's on your mind?"

"Okay, I'll come right to the point. I've got a chance to manage a high-class men's store in Nassau, in the Bahamas. One of my customers owns a string of stores, and he needs a new manager there. It's a great opportunity for me, but..."

"I know," Charlie interrupted, "what about your share of the gold?"

"Yeah. I don't think I should lose my share even though I have to leave Denver."

"You know, Tom, we were counting on you to help lug the bags of ore out of the cave. We can't expect the women to do it. Also, you were expected to help chip out that vein in the cave wall. What's your solution to that problem?"

"I, I, don't know. But I want my share. After all, I was there when we found it."

"You know I'll have to let another man in on the project, and he'll have to get a share. So here's what I propose. Since you won't be doing any of the work, we'll give you one-eighth of the net proceeds and expenses. How does that strike you?"

"But, Charlie..."

"No buts, Tom. That's fair and that's the way its got to be. Take it or leave it. You're causing us a lot of trouble. You go to Nassau, and we'll see that you get your one-eighth share."

"How do I know you'll keep your word?"

"You son of a bitch. I'm used to dealing with people whose word is their bond. If you can't accept my word then go get a lawyer and pay him to draw up a legal agreement. But I'm telling you right now that it better be a simple, straightforward document or none of the three of us will sign it."

"All right, all right. I can't afford a lawyer. I'll take your word for it."

"Not so fast. I'll draw up a simple agreement for all four of us to sign, and we'll have it notarized. Anything else you want to talk about?"

"Uh, no. I guess not."

"I'll let you know when its ready to sign. Goodbye."

With a glum, sour face Tom got up and left the office.

As the door closed, Charlie growled, "And good riddance." He leaned back with a smile on his face. Tom's leaving solves a problem. It doesn't create one. And he didn't have the guts to talk about Jean. I hope the people of Nassau can take his kind. Maybe they'll teach him some manners. I know just the man to replace the S.O.B. Jake! Has to be Jake.

11

PLANNING FOR THE GOLD

CHARLIE MIXED DRINKS FOR SHARON AND JEAN and poured a scotch and water for himself. They toasted Project Arrow.

"Well, ladies, you already know why Tom isn't here. I'm sure you'll agree with me that we won't miss him. He would have been big trouble up there at the waterfall. But we will have to replace him. There's too much hard work for just the three of us. I'd like to bring Jake, my mechanic, into the project. I know he's trustworthy, and we'll need his muscle. Is that okay with you, ladies?"

"Yes," they agreed in unison.

Jean added, "Good riddance. Tom's a lot more trouble than he's worth."

"I agree," Sharon confirmed.

"Okay," Charlie continued, "I've drafted an agreement that we all, including Tom, will sign. It gives him one-eighth of our net profit. We'll have to have a notary witness our signatures, but have Tom come separately so you two won't have to deal with him."

"Thanks, Charlie," Jean sighed.

"Now," Charlie emphasized, "we have to do some planning. We're close to our first flight back to the gold. I've got my helicopter pilot license, and I've decided on the chopper we need. Jean, is it okay if I lease it right away?"

"Of course. I'm anxious to get on with this adventure."

"Good. Our first flight will be primarily to stake out our claim. We'll also take some supplies and tools to leave there. Jake and I can handle this first flight. You ladies won't have to go."

"Oh no. Don't leave me out," Jean interjected. "I want to go and help."

"How about you, Sharon?"

"Well, it depends on when you're going."

"I'd like to go this coming Friday and return Sunday."

"Then I won't be able to make the trip, Dad. I have an important modeling assignment on Saturday."

"Okay. Then it's Jake, Jean, and me. I'll talk to Jake and brief him. He's eager to join us and is available most any time. We'll lift off at nine Friday morning."

"I'll be there, Charlie," Jean promised.

Charlie grinned at Jean and continued. "We'll take two pickaxes, two shovels, some canvas bags, two tents, and some canned foods to store up there. Jean, would you fix us enough food for three days in the wilderness? Simple, easy things."

"Sure."

"I'll help," Sharon added.

"Thank you, both of you. We'll also take six angle-iron posts for staking out the claim and a sledgehammer. Remember, we have to stake out a rectangular area four corner posts and one in the middle of each long side."

"Dad, how do we get the gold ore to Denver? Fly it back in the helicopter?"

"I'm glad you brought that up. I've been thinking about that and the problem we'll have with security and secrecy. My first thought is to fly the ore to Maher or Montrose and ship it from there by ground transport. Perhaps we could use Brinks or Wells Fargo security trucks. I don't know. Also, I have to find out where we can take the ore for refining or smelting, whatever the process is called. But our first order of business is staking our lode claim and filing it with the county recorder.

"Charlie," Jean interjected, "I just remembered the term used for cleaning the ore and separating the gold. It's called beneficiation."

"What would I do without you." Charlie beamed as he leaned forward and took her hand in his.

"I can't imagine," Jean purred with love in her eyes.

Sharon smiled at the two as she realized something serious was going on here.

Charlie slowly released Jean's hand, forced the doting look from his face, and became the business-like leader again. "When we come back from this first flight we have to bring some ore samples to be assayed. They have to be one-inch deep chips from the vein and weigh one to two pounds each. These chips will be analyzed to determine the value of the ore. Jean, where do we take the chips for assay?"

"The U. S. Bureau of Mines, Denver."

"Just checking to see if our cornucopia, our source of information, that's you Jean, is still brimful of everything we need."

"Dad, Jean has all you, ah, I mean, we will ever need." His daughter's mischievous smile revealed the true meaning of her words.

"Of course," Charlie agreed as he tried to regain a semblance of composure.

"Thank you, Sharon. I hope you are right in more ways than one. Now, where were we, the Bureau of Mines?" Jean questioned.

"Yeah, the Bureau of Mines. Let's leave that subject for now," Charlie advised, "and go, uh, back to supplies. Jake and I will get everything we need but the food and water. I guess that's all we need to talk about now. How about another drink, ladies?"

"Not me," Sharon answered as she rose from her chair. "I've got to get my beauty sleep. I have a busy day tomorrow."

"I'll have one," Jean murmured.

"Me too," Charlie said with a nervous cough.

"Good night, fellow gold seekers. See you tomorrow," Sharon called as she left the room.

"Charlie, you and Jake in one tent and me in the other one right next to yours. I'm afraid of bears."

"Yes. That's the right way, darn it. Don't worry about the wild life. I sleep lightly and can handle the bears."

"I better go. I think your daughter sees through our facade. Maybe we can get together sometime before we fly off to the mountains."

"I'll call you tomorrow. We'll plan a little rendezvous."

MIKE'S PLAN TO HEIST THE GOLD

Mike entered the hangar office through the window. No one had relocked it, and it slid up easily. It was two o'clock in the morning, and there was no activity around the hangars. He had parked in the same place he had before and walked to the hangar.

Following the bug guy's instructions, he went to a heating vent on an inside wall of the office. With a small screwdriver he removed the louvered vent cover. Just inside the vent he saw the receiver and a small voice-activated cassette recorder. He removed the tape and inserted a new one. After replacing the vent cover, he hurried back to the window. After making sure there was no one around to witness his exit, Mike climbed out the window, closed it, and walked back to his car.

An hour later he was in his apartment listening to the tape. Mike smiled as it ended and went to bed. He'd call Joey and Murph in the morning.

Joey and Murph arrived at Mike's apartment at eight o'clock the next evening. They had come together in Joey's car.

"Hi guys. Help yourself to the beer," Mike greeted them.

Joey took one look at the six-pack and exclaimed, "Hey, what is this beer? Kronigsbourg! Never heard of it."

"It's a special beer for celebrating good news, Joey."

Murph growled, "Some rotten foreign stuff. Right, Mike?"

"No, not rotten. You'll like it. It's expensive imported beer."

"What's with this celebration? What's the news?" Joey demanded.

Mike settled into his lounge chair and smiled. "Last night I got the tape from the hangar office. I'm not going to play it because there's a lot of garbage on it. But let me tell you, we got what we wanted."

"Out with it, man," Murph hissed.

"Cool it, Murph. There were four things in the conversation that confirm what we thought about this deal. First, the word gold was used. So we were right, they were talking about gold that night at the Rathskeller. Second, get this, they talked about riches in the mountains. I take that to mean they found gold somewhere up there."

"Hey, Mike, can I have another beer. This Kron somethin' is good," Murph interrupted. "You know me. I'm a buy American guy. No Nip or Kraut cars for me. But this brew is okay."

"Sure. Help yourself."

"Thanks."

"The third thing is Charlie talking about getting a helicopter license. Seems like they need a chopper to get to the gold. Charlie's the pilot and seems to be the leader of the group. Evidently there are four of them in on this deal. The last thing on the tape was talk about shares of the gold."

"So, we know they're after gold," Joey reasoned. "What's our next move?"

"I've been thinking about that. I…"

"Wait, Mike," Joey exclaimed. "What's the pilot's last name? Do you know it?"

"Yeah. It's on his flight plan I saw in the tower. It's Buckholtz. Why?"

"Because, remember the story in the newspapers a month or so ago about a small airplane crashing in the mountains. I think the pilot's name was Buckholtz. There were four people in the plane. They walked out of the forest. Remember that Murph?"

"Naw. I only read the comics and the editorial page. I like to read about how dumb and crooked our politicians are," Murph giggled.

"Hey," Mike said, "I remember that. You're right. The pilot was this Charlie. That means those people probably found gold up where they crashed or when they were hiking out."

"Man, we're getting close to the payoff," Murph screeched.

"Maybe," Mike cautioned. "Do you realize how tough it'll be to get heavy gold ore out of the mountains. Now, my idea is to let our suckers bring the gold out and then grab it. We'll have to keep checking on their moves and figure out a way to heist the gold from them once they've got it off the mountain."

Joey opened another beer. "We'll have to keep that bug and recorder in the hangar office. Any other way we can get information, Mike?"

"I think so. I have a buddy in the tower who will keep us informed on their flights, if I grease his palm. I'll check that recorder again after their next flight to the mountains and keep you guys informed. We'll figure a way to get that gold. Don't you worry."

"I don't worry 'bout nothin'," Murph sneered.

"See you later, guys. I gotta go," Joey said as he went to the door. Murph got up to join him.

"Remember, guys. No talkin' to anyone else about our project."

"Sure, Mike," Joey responded.

Murph, with a surly look, nodded his head.

ANOTHER FLIGHT TO GOLD

Charlie had the flight plan to the Arrow mine filed before Jean and Jake got to his office. The Eurocopter was on the tarmac in front of the hangar. Jean arrived fifteen minutes early.

"Good morning, Charlie."

"Morning, Jean. Are you ready for our trip over the mountains to the cave of gold?"

"Primed and eager. Notice my boots, jeans, and lumberjack shirt. I'm ready for camping in the wilderness."

"You look beautiful even in those kind of clothes."

"Thank you."

"Before Jake gets here I'll bring you up to date on other things. I got Tom's notarized signature on our agreement. He's leaving for Nassau tomorrow. Let's hope he's out of our lives for good now. Also, I've drawn up an agreement that includes Jake. He'll get one-eighth of the net profit. But I figure if we hit it big we could give him a bonus. How does that sound to you?"

"Sure. He'll be working hard for his share. And Charlie, I hope you won't over do it on the heavy work."

"I'll be careful. You don't need to worry about me."

Jake came in from the hangar. "Hi, Charlie. Hello, Mrs. Prescott. How'd you like your ride in the WACO?"

"It was exciting. I loved it. Jake, now that we're partner's in this gold venture, please call me Jean."

"Okay, Jean. Charlie, the chopper is ready."

"Good. Now, let me brief you two about this flight. First, Jean, you might be interested in some facts about this helicopter. Jake already knows. It's a Eurocopter with two Pratt and Whitney engines. It has a range of 356 miles and cruises at 139 knots. It can hold six passengers and lift six thousand pounds. Jake took out two of the seats for more cargo space. All the supplies are loaded, including six five-gallon cans of emergency fuel that we'll leave at the waterfall."

"Sounds good to me," Jean affirmed.

"We'll be lifting off in twenty minutes. The weather looks good except for light wind in the mountains, which will produce some unwanted wave turbulence. The straight-line mileage to the mine site is 143 miles, but zigzagging through passes and valleys to get around the peaks will add to that. I figure it'll be closer to 180 miles before we reach our destination. I've allowed for extra time and fuel consumption to find the chopper pad."

"Our first landmark is Red Hill Pass at ten thousand feet. Then comes Weston Pass at twelve thousand feet. About twenty more miles on our highway in the sky and, weather permitting, we'll fly between two peaks. The one off to starboard is Mount Elbert Peak, the highest peak in Colorado. On our port side we'll see La Plata Peak. A few miles farther is the town of Crested Butte where there's an airport, our first alternate airfield in case of deteriorating weather. Next is Kebler Pass to starboard and Ohio Peak to port. Then it's only about ten miles to our destination.

"Sounds like you've figured everything," Jake reasoned.

"Yes," Jean added. "I'm glad we have the extra time and fuel we might need to locate the landing site."

Charlie continued. "There are two alternate airfields if we need them, one at the little town of Crawford, the other at Montrose. Any questions?"

"No questions. Let's go," Jean answered.

"Yeah. I'm ready," Jake agreed.

"One more thing, Jake. What did you tell your wife about this trip?"

"Only what you told me to say, that Jean wants to build a retreat there. Darrae likes the extra money I bring in."

"Darrae. Is that your wife's given name?" Jean asked.

"Yes. Unusual isn't it? Her mother got it from a book."

"It's a lovely name."

"Jake," Charlie advised, "if your wife can keep a secret, I guess it's okay to tell her about this project. I think it's only right."

"She can keep secrets, even from me. Thanks."

"Okay. Let's go!"

The Eurocopter rose from the tarmac right on schedule. Charlie turned to 260 degrees and started climbing. By the time they saw Red Hill Pass the altitude was eleven thousand feet. A few isolated clouds scudded the mountains, but visibility was excellent. They cleared the rocky peak by a thousand feet. The sky was still clear at Weston Pass, and they enjoyed the view of the towering mountain walls as they flew by.

In the distance, Mount Elbert and La Plata peaks were visible. Ominous clouds draped the peaks as if standing guard to prevent the chopper from continuing south. Charlie thought if there ever was a place for downdrafts and mountain wave turbulence, that's it.

"We're not going between those two peaks ahead. There could be strong down draft, too strong. We're going around La Plata Peak instead and then get back on course," Charlie announced.

"Good idea," Jake agreed.

"Those clouds on the peaks are dangerous?" Jean asked.

"You got that right, Jean," Charlie confirmed.

The air became rougher as they proceeded around La Plata, making it necessary for Charlie to constantly adjust the power and lift of the helicopter. Still they bounced up and down like a yo-yo. Charlie increased altitude to just beneath the clouds. At thirteen thousand feet, they were near the service ceiling of the helicopter and the controls were responding slowly.

Turning back to their original heading, Charlie fought the unseen power of the wind turbulence until they cleared the mountains and the terrain below became a lush green valley.

"We're going to a lower altitude now," Charlie told his passengers. "Should be smoother air down there. Before long we'll see Crested Butte where we can land and refuel. We have to tank up before the return trip to Centennial. Might as well be on the safe side and get it done now."

As they approached the Crested Butte airfield, Jake said, "There's the fueling area just right of twelve o'clock, Charlie."

"I see it. Down we go. We'll stretch our legs and get some coffee. Then it's off to our camp site and gold mine."

In the air again, heading south-southwest, Charlie informed his passengers, "I see Kebler Pass and Ohio Peak ahead. We fly through the pass with the peak on our left and then it's only about ten miles. The air was surprisingly smooth as they went by Ohio Peak towering above them. Charlie began a descent. "Jean, look for the waterfall and the rock cliff. We're almost over the right area now."

"Okay. Bet I spot them before you do."

They descended to five thousand feet above the terrain, and Charlie banked into a tight search orbit.

"Maybe I'll spot one of those landmarks before either one of you do," Jake challenged.

"Fat chance," Charlie laughed as he widened the orbit.

"Look! There's the rock wall at about ten o'clock," Jean shouted.

Charlie turned to port immediately and spotted the wall. "Good job, Jean. We should see our landing pad in a couple of minutes," Charlie said with satisfaction. A minute later Charlie spotted the clearing. "There it is straight ahead. Goin' down now for a nice, smooth touchdown."

From four thousand feet, the clearing looked about the size of a postage stamp. Charlie started the descent, jockeying the chopper back and forth as it slowly dropped down into the tiny clearing. A slight wind required precise control. They touched down in the center of the now enlarged postage stamp.

"Charlie, you're a master helicopter pilot," Jean said, beaming with admiration.

"Right on," Jake agreed.

"Thanks. Let's get unloaded."

12

STAKING THE CLAIM

THEY SET UP THE TENTS NEAR THE HELICOPTER, put the gas cans in the woods near the edge of the clearing, and stored the other supplies next to the tents. Charlie noticed Jean frequently looking around at the forest. He knew she had bears on her mind and maybe mountain lions too. He did when he looked at his scarred arm.

"It's too late to do any work today," Charlie told Jake and Jean. "So let's go down to the river and show Jake our claim. Then we'll build a cook fire, have dinner, and get to bed early. Follow us, Jake." Charlie smiled as he took Jean's hand.

At the riverbank Jean asked Jake, "Do you see anything sparkling in the water?"

"I guess you mean nuggets, right Jean? The sun must be too low. I can't see any gold."

"Jake," Charlie interrupted, "look to your right at the waterfall. See anything odd about it?"

"Hmm. Looks like a standard waterfall to me."

"Look at the very center of the face, about half way up."

"Oh, I see what you mean. The spray isn't white, looks gray and dirty."

"Any idea what that means?" Jean asked.

"Nope, I guess I'm not the experienced outdoors type like you two."

"Jake," Charlie advised, "that's where the gold is. That dark area in the spray is the mouth of a cave behind the waterfall. Tomorrow you'll see it. Let's go back now and have a picnic dinner."

"Wait just a minute, Charlie. You got me all excited about seeing gold, and now you expect me to go picnicking. Come on, boss, there's plenty of daylight left. I want to see the gold now, not tomorrow."

"Jake's right, Charlie," Jean implored. "I'm anxious to see it again too."

"Okay, you two. I'm outnumbered. But first, let's get a lantern, a pickax, and a couple of canvas bags to leave in the cave ready for tomorrow. Remember though, our first job in the morning is to stake out the claim. Come on, let's go."

Charlie led them up the riverbank to the falls. "Jake, see that narrow, slippery ledge. It's the only way to get to the cave. I'll go first, then Jean. Watch your step. Be prepared to get wet. Come on, Jean. Hold my hand."

Facing the rock wall, they cautiously made their way along the ledge to the cave entrance. When Jake entered he asked, "How did you find this, Charlie?"

"After the Arrow crash we came by here on our way out of the forest. I saw that dark spot in the waterfall and my curiosity took over. I had to see what it was. Look at this wall, Jake." Charlie held up the lantern and the whole cave was illuminated.

Jake looked closely and ran his hand along the glittering vein.

"Good God, Charlie It sure looks promising. You're sure it isn't pyrite fool's gold?"

"I'm sure. I can tell the difference. Pyrite is more yellow than gold. Look over here at this pile of rocks. They're streaked with gold. Someone found this mother lode, chipped them out, and left them here a long time ago. We found this old miner's pickaxe here, and it's from the late eighteen hundreds. Whoever found this place apparently never got back to cash in on his discovery."

"Man, sure looks like we've hit it big. I'm anxious to chip out some of that vein. Wonder how big it is?"

"No tellin' Jake, until we start work on it. Come on. Now you've seen it, let's get some chow and a good night's sleep."

In the morning, after a peaceful night, they sipped their coffee as Charlie told Jean and Jake his plan for the day. "Our first job is to stake out the claim. We'll start above the waterfall. We take two of the iron stakes and the signs that attach to them and the small sledgehammer. About thirty feet upstream of the falls we place the stakes fifty feet out from the center line of the falls, one on each side of the river directly across from each other."

They started out through the dense underbrush and trees, so thick it was impossible to walk a straight line. Charlie led the way up past the waterfall, pacing off thirty feet, and looked back where the river dropped out of sight. The spray of the waterfall was still visible. "Okay, fifty feet from the middle of the river."

Jake hammered the first stake into the ground and attached the claim sign. It read, "Arrow Claim, August 6, 1997."

Back at the river Charlie found a possible crossing. "Here we go. There are a few flat rocks and it's not too deep. But water is running fast and the rocks will be slippery. We need to hold hands. I'll go first, then Jean, then Jake."

As they reached the middle of the torrent, Jean slipped and started to fall. Jake slipped too and lost his grip on Jean's hand but managed to keep his balance. Jean dropped into the water, but Charlie clung to her hand and pulled her back to him against the fierce flow of water above the waterfall. Jean was soaking wet as Charlie hauled her up against him.

"You all right, Jean?"

Dripping water she sputtered, "Soaked and frozen with a skinned knee. Thanks, Charlie. I thought I'd be swept over the falls. That current is so strong, I was terrified."

"Can't have you going over the falls, darling. I need you."

"Sorry, Jean, " Jake blustered. "I slipped and lost my grip on you."

"Let's go," Charlie urged. "We'll get this other stake in and get you back to camp to fix that skinned knee and into some dry clothes.

After pounding in the other stake and attaching the claim sign, they re-crossed the river and returned to camp. Jean tended to her knee and got into some dry clothes. She agreed to stay in her tent while Charlie and Jake went to install the other four stakes. The men were back by eleven o'clock ready for an early lunch.

After eating in record time, Jake said excitedly, "I'm hungry for gold now. Let's go back to the cave."

THE CAVE OF DEATH

Mike sipped a beer as he watched a Broncos football game on television with his girlfriend, Amy, next to him drinking white wine. Every time she asked Mike a question about the game, Mike would drone out the answers and wish she'd shut up. She was distracting him, and it was getting tiresome. The phone rang and agitated him even more.

"Hello, Mike here." He listened intently then said, "Right. Thanks. In the mail tomorrow." He slowly hung up the phone. His no-name tower guy had just told him about Buckholtz's departure for Crested Butte yesterday in a helicopter. Mike would send a check tomorrow.

"Come on, babe, let's go out. It's the fourth quarter and the Broncos are twenty points ahead. They've got it made. A couple of drinks then back here for fun and games."

"Not another TV game, I hope."

"You know what I mean."

"Yeah. Right on."

The azure sky directly overhead was speckled by small white clouds slowly traversing north to south. Even so, Charlie could see trouble coming as he gazed at the mountain peaks and the clouds. Some of the cumulus clouds were massing into gray nimbus rain formations. When these clouds flattened into an anvil shape, thunderstorms were inevitable. It would be a wet day. Charlie thought it would be smart to tie down the helicopter and move their tents to higher ground

They were so eager to get to the cave that breakfast was only crackers and coffee. Charlie told Jean and Jake what to expect from the ominous clouds. After tying down the helicopter and moving the tents, they began their trek to the waterfall. Slowly and cautiously they made their way along the narrow ledge to the cave. Once inside Charlie turned on the battery-powered lantern.

"Our first job," Charlie advised, "is to go through the pile of rocks and put the ones with only specks of gold in one pile and the ones with streaks of gold in another. We'll take the streaked rocks out later. The speckled ones aren't worth bothering with.

"When do we start chipping away at the vein?" Jake asked.

"This afternoon. Jake you start sorting on this side of the pile. Jean and I'll do the other."

For the next half hour, Jean worked pulling rocks aside while Charlie separated them.

Suddenly Jean let out a piercing scream and fell back away from the rocks into the wall.

"Jean, what is it? What's happened?" Charlie said as he knelt beside her.

"Look, over here by the wall. It's, oh God, it's a human skull."

"My God, I see it."

Jake hurried over to see. "Sure does looks like a skull."

Charlie helped Jean away from the grisly sight to the mouth of the cave. "Sit here. I'll get you some water."

Jake started pulling rocks away from the wall near the skull. He quickly uncovered more of the skeleton. Charlie joined him saying, "No more sorting rocks. Let's get the rocks off the rest of the bones."

Jean stayed near the mouth of the cave, trying to regain some composure, while Charlie and Jake uncovered the skeleton. Among the bones and shreds of clothing, Charlie found a metal belt buckle with the name Buck etched in it.

"I assume this guy's name was Buck," Charlie said as he put the buckle in his pocket." Charlie peered intently at bones. "Jake, this man was stabbed in the back. There's the knife between two ribs." The handle of the knife was outside the rib cage. Taking the double-edged knife out from under the skeleton, Charlie examined it closely. The brass handle was engraved "Springfield 1843." "That ties in with the age of that old pick and supports my theory that this happened in the eighteen hundreds," Charlie said as he turned away and went to Jean.

"Would you like to go back to camp? We've done plenty of work."

"No, Charlie, I'm all right. We came here to chip pieces out that vein. Let's get some of that done. Then we can get out of here."

"Okay. As you wish." Charlie turned to Jake. "Get a canvas bag for all the bones, and we'll give this poor guy a decent burial."

Charlie picked up the small pickaxe and began chipping at the vein. It was fairly easy to get two-inch chunks because there was so much soft gold in the ore. He had collected several pieces of gold ore by the time Jake had completed his macabre task,

"Jean, Jake, come here and feel the weight of these pieces. They're loaded with gold. That's why they're so heavy for their size. I've only cut in about an inch and the vein is still packed with gold."

Jean took a piece in her hand. "Wow! It's beautiful. Did we bring scales to weigh them on?"

"That's an item we don't have here," Charlie answered.

"Sure looks like we're into the mother lode here," Jake said.

Charlie put the ore pieces in a canvas bag, saying, "Let's go. Bring the sack of bones, Jake. It's time for us to get out of this hell hole."

Jean sat down with a sigh and said, "I need a drink. I brought my bourbon and your scotch, Charlie. What'll you have, Jake?"

"I'll have one of my beers."

They relaxed as Jean fixed the drinks and Jake opened his beer.

"I've got a theory," Charlie mused, "about what happened to that poor guy in the cave. I think he and a partner found the gold and then had a falling out. You know, gold and greed are bedfellows, like in that movie *The Treasure of Sierra Madre* with Humphrey Bogart. Anyway, I figure Buck was killed and covered up with rocks by his partner. The partner probably went to stake his claim and never made it back."

"Sounds reasonable to me," Jake agreed. "That knife must have gone into his heart, I guess."

"Poor soul," Jean whispered. "And you think it all happened back in the eighteen hundreds, Charlie?"

"I'm sure of it. The old pickaxe we found, the belt buckle, and the dated knife."

"Enough," Jean yawned. "I'm going to have a siesta and forget all this horror. What can you two do that's quiet?"

"If we don't get a thunderstorm, Jake and I will bury Buck. If we get a hard rain, all three of us should get into the chopper to keep dry. Get some rest, Jean. I'll wake you up if we have to move into the chopper. Come on, Jake, bring the sack. I'll get the shovel."

As they walked toward the river, Charlie looked to the sky. "The thunderheads are a mountain range away to the west. We might get lucky and get only a light shower if they continue on their present course."

In a small clearing thirty feet from the river, Jake started digging and four feet down hit solid rock.

"That'll have to be deep enough," Charlie said. They covered the remains with dirt and topped the grave with rocks.

Charlie stepped back and bowed his head. "Rest in peace, Buck."

JEAN'S SURPRISE

Charlie's prediction for good weather came true. The storm stayed to the west drenching the next mountain range and valley while only a light sprinkle fell on them. Jean woke from her siesta at three o'clock.

"Jake, lay a cook fire. I want to show Jean where we buried Buck." It was a pretty slim excuse to be alone with Jean, but it was the best he could do. He was sure Jake would understand.

Hand in hand they ambled slowly to the river and downstream to the small clearing. "Those stones aren't much of a marker for Buck, but it's the best we could do."

"In this rustic setting it's fine, Charlie. Let's go down to the river and watch the sun set behind the mountains." They sat on a grassy knoll silently communing with the sun, the mountains, and the rushing river.

"Charlie, I've been thinking. Are we crazy rushing into a project like this when we don't have to? I know it's been a thrilling adventure and could be financially rewarding, but is it worth the risks? I'm beginning to wonder if we're doing the right thing."

"Jean, I'm surprised. I thought you were a hundred percent into this project."

"I was at the start. But let me finish telling you what I've been thinking. As you know, I'm a wealthy woman. Of course, I have people who manage all my assets, but I've grown tired of this burden of wealth and long for a different life, the simple, uncomplicated life of just being with you. I love you. I need you. And I believe you feel the same way about me." Jean raised her steady gaze at the river and turned to Charlie. Their lips met in a long, ardent kiss.

Charlie broke their embrace and looked lovingly into her eyes. "You're so right, Jean. I do love you and need you. I would do anything for you. Of course, about all I have to offer you are my home, my airplane, and all my love for the rest of our lives."

"Oh, Charlie, that's all I need or want. Knowing that you love me and that we can fly away now and then in the WACO makes me happy. I don't need my jet, I don't even want it now that I've flown in an open cockpit plane."

"But, Jean, what will you do with all your holdings?"

"I've thought about that too. I'll give my son a share, but most of the proceeds from the sale of my assets will go to the charities I care most about. I'll keep three million in our names, the interest will give us plenty to live on. Do you have any organizations you'd like to support?"

"Yes, I do. Disabled American Veterans and a museum in Normandy, France."

"A museum in France. You must have a special reason for that."

"I do. I had an older brother who was killed on D-Day at Omaha

Beach in Normandy. The museum is in Caen and is called The Battle of Normandy Memorial Museum. I contributed to the building of it."

"I can see that you feel the loss of your brother deeply, Charlie. I'd like to contribute too."

"That's generous of you, Jean. I'm sure the museum will appreciate your contribution. Let's talk more about your idea when we get back home. It's a major step in your life."

"I know, but I'm sure it's a step in the direction I want to travel."

"I understand, but let's go back to camp now. Despite your startling revelations, I have a hearty appetite for our campfire dinner."

Jake was nowhere in sight, but the dinner fire was ready to light and cans of beans and corned beef hash were on a log nearby.

"Listen, Jean." Charlie pointed to the tent from which light snores were emanating.

"I hear it. Let's start dinner and wake him when it's ready."

"Good idea. I'll start the fire."

After their sumptuous wilderness dinner, they enjoyed hot coffee.

"We'll leave tomorrow after breakfast," Charlie advised. "We have enough samples of ore to be assayed. And I can fly to the county seat of Gunnison County to file and register our claim the day after tomorrow. Is my WACO ready to fly, Jake?"

"Don't know. Have to check a couple of things. Probably will be ready."

Jean rose from her log seat and announced, "I'm going to bed. Let's get up early and get out of this wilderness. I need a shower and a juicy steak dinner. Good night."

"Good idea. G'night," Charlie agreed.

Charlie's eyes opened instantly and his hand slid to his pistol at the sound of a twig cracking. He eased silently out of his bedroll. Jake was sound asleep, snoring lightly. He paused at the tent flaps to part them slightly and peered into the night. The half moon in a cloudless sky dimly lit the clearing. He couldn't see any movement but knew something was out there and decided to get a better look.

He crept slowly out of the tent and crouching low moved only his head to look around. He looked at Jean's tent, then scanned the clearing. Nothing. Cautiously he moved around behind the tent and surveyed the other half of the clearing.

To his left a slight movement in the aspens caught his attention, and he stared at the trees about one hundred feet away. There was no wind to make them quake. Something, some animal must be there. Charlie aimed his pistol at the trees and stood motionless. A full two minutes passed before the branches parted and revealed a brown bear entering the clearing. The bear stopped suddenly and stared at Charlie. The huge beast stood up and opened his mouth and roared. Huge yellowed teeth accented the gaping maw. The power of those terrible jaws could crush bones.

Suddenly it dropped to all fours and with a fearsome growl, rushed Charlie. He stood his ground and took aim knowing he had only three or four seconds to get off a shot, a deadly shot, between the eyes. The bear was charging at full speed as Charlie pulled the trigger. The shot struck the bear squarely between the eyes and the monster collapsed almost at Charlie's feet..

Jake dashed out of his tent. "What happened, Charlie?"

Before Charlie could answer, Jean rushed from her tent. "What was that shot, Charlie? What... Oh, my God!" she screamed as she stared at the huge dead animal.

"Looks like you got him just in time," Jake said with awe.

"Yeah, sure does."

"Oh, Charlie, are you all right?" Jean asked in a shaking voice.

"I'm okay. Our visitor didn't appreciate that we have been trespassing in his territory."

"Well, I don't want us to be here either. Let's pack up and get out of here now," Jean pleaded.

"I know how you feel Jean, but we can' t do that. It's too dangerous to fly the mountains at night. We'll leave first thing in the morning."

"Nice shot, Charlie, you got him right between the eyes," Jake said. "I'm going back to bed."

"Me too," Charlie concurred. "Jean, try to get some sleep. We'll be okay. No more bears around tonight."

"I'll try. But this is one more reason for having second thoughts about the project. My God, Charlie, that beast nearly got to you." Jean moaned.

"I'll be ready at first light. Good night again."

13

MIKE AND JOEY GET CLOSER

A SOLID OVERCAST OF GRAY CLOUDS flowing slowly over the peaks of the mountains west of the airfield obscured the sky. The clouds were not dark enough to be a rain threat, but that could change quickly.

Mike and Joey relaxed in Mike's car parked where they could see the runway of Centennial Airport. The line of hangars was also in their view. They had sandwiches and a cooler filled with iced cans of beer.

"Ready for a brew, Mike?"

"Yeah, ready. The chopper's due in half an hour. Hope those clouds over the mountains don't delay Buckholtz's flight."

Charlie fought the turbulence in Weston Pass. They had left the woods at nine that morning. There were dark clouds near the mountaintops, but Charlie knew they could fly through the passes and over the valleys.

"Charlie," Jean moaned, "get us on the ground soon. This rough air is getting to my stomach."

"Okay, Jean. Only one more pass to get through. Jake, get her an air-sick bag. They're in the door pocket."

"Here, Jean." Jake smiled. "Just in case."

Charlie added more power to try slicing through the turbulence with less bouncing around. They came out of the pass into smoother air.

"There's Red Hill Pass ahead. Beyond that it'll be clear sailin' to Centennial. Hang in there."

Jean didn't answer as she clutched the bag.

Mike and Joey were into their second beers when Mike checked the time again.

"This waiting is for the birds!" Joey groaned.

"I know, but someone has to do it," Mike laughed.

"It's almost eleven now. Time for the bird to be here. Look at those clouds, they're getting lower. Maybe our boy won't make it."

"Patience, man. He'll show up. My man in the tower got his flight plan."

They peered intently through the windshield as a twin engine Beechcraft in the western sky was lining up with the runway. Wavering back and forth, the pilot crabbed into the wind and straightened out as the wheels touched down.

"Nice landing in that crosswind," Mike remarked.

"Look up there toward the mountains," Joey exclaimed. "Maybe that's the chopper."

Silently they focused on the speck in the sky.

"That's a chopper!" Mike exclaimed loudly. "Not many come in here. I bet it's our guy. We have to watch where he sets down. If it's at hangar eight, he's our man."

The helicopter roared over the runway in front of Mike and Joey and turned toward the hangars.

Charlie hovered a hundred feet above the tarmac in front of his hangar. "When we set down, Jean, you go unlock the side door and wait for me in the office. Give her the key, Jake. You and I'll get these heavy bags into the hangar first, then our luggage." The helicopter settled slowly onto the ground and Charlie shut down the engines.

"Come on Jake. Let's get all this stuff into the hangar. I'll lock the chopper."

After Charlie got off the phone closing out his flight plan, he said, "Jake, we'll put everything in your car. No space for it in my little MG. You know where my house is. Jean and I will follow and unload all our stuff there before you go on home to Darrae. How are you doin', Jean?"

"Much better now that we're on good old terra firma."

"See that, Joey. They're draggin' those bags into the hangar. Guess why?"

"Yeah. I know what would make them so heavy. Gold!"

"You got that right. We'll follow them and see where they go from here. I'll lay ya two to one those bags won't stay in the hangar tonight."

"Right on."

Forty-five minutes later Mike turned off the headlights and parked a block away from the two cars they had followed. He and Joey watched as Jake's car was unloaded.

"There go the gold bags into the house," Mike muttered. "Too bad we don't have a bug in there."

"Right. So, what's our next move?" Joey asked.

"We'll wait a few minutes then drive by the house and get the address."

"I mean when do we go after the gold?"

"We don't, not until they've brought out more gold. There's not much in those two bags. Look, one of them is leaving. Now, let's get that house number."

"Eight twenty-three," Joey noted as they passed the house. "Melrose Avenue. Let's go to the Rathskeller and have a boilermaker to celebrate."

"I'm all for that."

SHARON' S SURPRISE

"I'm exhausted, Charlie," Jean sighed. "I'm going home and soak for an hour in the bathtub before I fix myself a juicy filet and go to bed. Too bad you have to stay here and guard our gold."

"I know what happened last night and the flight today has been rough on you. Hope you feel better tomorrow. I'm tired too." Charlie drew her to him and kissed her lightly. "I'll call you in the morning."

"I love you, Charlie. Good night."

Charlie fixed a scotch and water and plopped down in his recliner.

The tension of the last two days seeped out of his body, and he thought only of Jean. *How could such a lovely woman settle for a gimpy old flyboy like me*, he wondered. *God, I do love her.*

The opening of the front door shook him out of his reverie.

"Hi, Dad. I see you finally got home. What's in those canvas bags in the hallway?"

"Hi, princess. The gold ore samples for assaying."

"Oh, of course. Tell me all about the trip, especially how Jean survived in the wilderness."

Charlie related the details minimizing the encounter with the bear. "How did things go with you while we were away?"

"The fashion show went smoothly, and I started designing a new ad campaign for wedding dresses. Could you give me some input on one of my ideas."

"Me, an old codger, advising on women's fashions? You're kidding."

"I'm serious, Dad. Listen to this. For a change, I want to include men in the ads for wedding dresses. I'd like the ad to show that men appreciate beautiful gowns too. What do you think?"

"I think I'll have another scotch and forget that you seem to think I know something about the advertising business and wedding dresses."

"Dad, I'm sincere. I want your advice. I'll fix your drink. I know how you like it. You sit there and think."

"Oh, God! What power a woman, especially a daughter, wields over a man. I might as well admit defeat and start the rusty wheels in my head turning."

Charlie slumped deeper into his chair. Just like her mother, he thought, and just as beautiful.

As his daughter returned with his drink, Charlie straightened up and sighed. "My darling daughter, you already have the answer. You don't need my incredibly nimble brain."

"What do you mean?"

"You said it yourself, the answer."

"I said it? What?"

"You want to show that men appreciate beautiful wedding dresses. There's your answer. You show a gentleman in the background or off to the side smiling appreciatively at the bride. He could even be reaching out to touch the woman and the dress."

"Genius, pure genius, father. I should have thought of that. It's perfect. You do have a nimble brain. I can picture it now, a suave gentlemen showing subtle, but unmistakable, desire for the bride in a gorgeous gown. Thank you for your brilliant insight."

"It was nothing, my dear. When prodded I can do it every day. Ha!"

"There's something else I want to talk to you about, Dad."

"Okay. Now I'm in the mood to listen to all your problems."

"Not a problem. It's more of, ah, an update on my life. I met an interesting man at the fashion show. He was there with his sister who is a buyer for a department store. After the show he waited for me and introduced himself. He pilots a corporate jet all over the country for the executives of a big electronics company. Of course I told him my father was a pilot and that you have a WACO."

"And did you tell him I had flown jets too?"

"No. We didn't get into your biography. Anyway, he invited me to dinner that evening." Sharon paused.

"And?"

"We had dinner at Le Brittany, and he said he'll call me next Thursday when he returns from a flight."

"Sounds like you're, shall we say, getting involved."

"Well, maybe. He's very charming and a real gentleman and wants a ride in your WACO. Would you take him for a short flight?"

"Sure. I'm anxious to meet your new friend. Now, I'm going to bed. It's been a long day." Charlie struggled out of his recliner.

"Me too. I'm bushed. Goodnight, Dad."

"Good night, princess."

THE MAP

Charlie went to the hangar early the next morning. On his desk was a note from Jake. "I'll be working in hangar five. Call me if you need anything." After a careful study of his maps, Charlie decided he didn't want to fly the WACO to Gunnison and decided to charter a flight. He made a call and arranged to have a plane ready in an hour.

Then he called Chet. "Hi. I'm through with your chopper. It needs fuel. Include that on my bill. The flight was great, no problems. I'll let you know when I need it again. So long."

He waited until nine o'clock to phone Jean. A sleepy voice murmured, "Go away."

"Oh, Jean, I'm sorry. Thought you'd be up by now."

"Charlie, good morning. I'm up," she cooed. "How are you?"

"Rested and ready to fly. I decided to charter a flight to Gunnison to file our claim. What was the name we decided on?"

"Arrow, Charlie, for your airplane."

"Oh yes. How would you like to go with me? We take off in about an hour."

"No, thanks. I'll wait for a ride in your WACO."

"Okay. I should be back by six o'clock. Did you have a good soak last night?"

"Sure did, it was heavenly. Call me when you get back."

"I will, my love. Bye."

"Bye. I love you."

Jake came in as Charlie put down the phone. "Hi, Charlie. I'm finished down at hangar five. Want me to check out the WACO now?"

"No. I'm not flying today. I'm going to Gunnison on a charter to file the claim. Have you seen any more of that nosy guy who was curious about our flights?"

"No, haven't seen him. Why? Is something buggin' you?"

"No, but we've got to be careful. I don't like the idea of someone nosing around. For the sake of security we might want to use another airfield when we bring out the gold. We'll talk more when I get back. I've got to go meet my charter now."

"Okay. See you later."

Charlie's trip to Gunnison sealed their ownership of the Arrow claim. He returned to Centennial at six that evening and went home to call Jean.

At two o'clock in the morning, Mike sneaked into Charlie's office to retrieve a cassette tape and put in a new one. Taking advantage of the opportunity Charlie's unlocked desk drawers presented, he checked to see if there was any new information. In the lower left drawer was a marked map. He took it and spread it out on the desk. A penciled line meandered from Denver through the mountains to Ohio Peak where there was an X marked inside a circle. The X was in Gunnison National Forest.

Mike took a small notebook from his pocket and copied names and the approximate location of the X in relation to Ohio Peak. He put the map back in the drawer exactly as he had found it and left the office, locking the door. Then it was a quick walk back to his car and home.

Mike called Maury, the bartender at the Rathskeller bar and grill, to reserve the back room for Saturday night from eight to ten.

Mike, Joey, and Murph entered the bar, got their drinks and went to the back room. Mike opened his briefcase and removed the cassette tape player and a map. "Listen to this tape, guys. I've started it at the point where it's interesting." They listened intently and silently.

"Great!" Joey crowed, "That confirms they found a gold mine."

"Yeah," Murph giggled.

Mike interjected sharply, "You're right. But there's a problem too. That guy Charlie's a shrewd, careful son of a bitch. Notice the talk about a nosy guy and using another airfield."

"Yeah, he's sharp," Joey affirmed. "Who's the nosy guy, Mike? You?"

"Of course. Now I'll have to stay away from there during the day."

As Murph sipped his beer, a scowl hardened his face. "I'll take that guy out anytime you want, Mike."

"Cool it, Murph. We won't have to do that. But I've been thinking we may have to change our plan. I don't like the possibility of them sneaking the gold out to an unknown airfield. We may have to figure a way to get to the mine."

"Is that why you have that map?" Joey asked.

"Yeah. Here look at it. I drew this myself from a map I found in Charlie's office. See the circled X. I'll bet you that's where the gold is."

"So that's why they used a chopper. There's no roads out in that wilderness," Murph grinned.

"You got that right," Joey agreed.

"I figure," Mike continued, "they've got a clearing big enough for the helicopter, and that's how they'll bring out the gold. Another clue one of the tapes said there was a rock cliff with no trees on it that they used as a navigation marker. We could charter a helicopter and look for a clearing near a bare cliff in the area marked with the X."

"Yeah, but where do we find a chopper with a pilot who'll keep his trap shut?" Murph sneered.

"Good question. I might have the answer. I know a guy who might help us out, but it'll cost plenty of dough or a cut of the action. I'll check him out and let you guys know. Now let's get out of here." Mike pushed back his chair and stood up. "Remember, keep your traps shut about this."

14

THE GOLD AND THE RING

THE NEXT DAY CHARLIE LOADED THE ORE samples into the trunk of his MG and drove to Jean's house. She was waiting for him on the porch and smiled radiantly as he approached.

"Good morning, Charlie. I'm ready. Where are we going?"

"The Bureau of Mines to drop off our ore samples, then lunch at Courtine's. Thought you'd enjoy French cuisine."

"Sounds great. But surely you couldn't fit all of the big sacks in the tiny trunk of this car."

"You're right. I'm only taking samples from the vein, not from the pile."

"Oh, that makes sense. Tell me, did all go well in Gunnison?"

"Oh sure. No problems. Our claim is filed and recorded. It's ours to work. We own it. And it was a nice flight, too. Buckle up. We're off to find out how rich our ore is."

At the Bureau of Mines, Charlie lugged a small canvas bag containing the pieces of ore up the steps with Jean beside him. He opened the door of the Assayer's Office, stopped abruptly, and nearly shouted at the man behind the desk "Olie, Oliver Tremaine. What's an old sea-dog like you doing behind a desk?" Jean edged into room behind Charlie.

"Charlie Buckholtz, the fly-boy. I ask you too, what brings you here?"

"Olie, this is my dear friend, Jean Prescott. Jean, Oliver, my life saver."

"Pleased to meet you, Oliver. What's this about life saver?"

"Charlie is exaggerating as usual. He's..."

"Let me tell the story," Charlie interrupted as he strode to the desk and placed the bag on the floor. "Olie sailed his ship into some miserable weather to pick me up after my F-86 was shot down. I had to eject over the Sea of Japan and the helicopter aboard his ship plucked me out of the water. I was almost frozen when he picked me up. Olie did save my life."

"I'm sure glad you did, Olie," Jean murmured. "Charlie means a lot to me."

Oliver looked at Jean and Charlie silently for a few seconds and asked, "Do I detect a budding romance here?"

"You could say that," Charlie agreed. "Right, Jean?"

With a shy blush, Jean agreed. "Yes, Charlie."

"Olie, are you the person I leave these gold ore samples with?" He placed the bag on Olie's desk.

"No, but I'll get them to the lab for you. Don't tell me you're a prospector now?"

"Not really. Jean and I stumbled into a, what shall I say, a find."

"Don't tell me any more, Charlie. I don't want to know. I'll get your ore to the lab and have a report for you in about four days. Give me your address and phone number. I'll fill out the form for you."

"Thanks, Olie. We're going to lunch now. Can you join us?"

"Nope. Got to slave away here. But we'll get together soon and rehash war stories. And you must bring your lovely lady."

"Yeah, let's do that. And thanks again for pullin' me out of the drink."

"Twas nothin'. I'll call you. See you later."

"Right. Leave a message if I'm not home."

"Nice to meet you, Oliver. I'd love to hear your war stories." Jean smiled.

Oliver grinned and turned back to his work.

Courtine's was a combination of real and faux French. The walls were covered with paintings of well-known Paris scenes. The waiter spoke few words of French, but the chef was French and knew the cuisine. Charlie and Jean were delighted with both the food and atmosphere.

They shared a bottle of Chardonnay with their light lunch.

Charlie raised his glass. “Look through the wine into my eyes.”

Jean touched her glass to Charlie’s and gazed into the wine. Suddenly she gasped, “There’s something in my…Charlie, is that a ring in my glass?”

“A ring? How could a ring get into your glass?”

“You rascal.” She reached into the wine glass and retrieved the diamond ring. “What a lovely ring. Thank you, Charlie.”

“My dear, Jean, that’s an engagement ring. I love you, and I’m asking you to marry me.”

“Oh Charlie, yes. I would love to be your wife.

“Let’s go back to my house for, as you say, a bit of etc. and I’ll show you how much I love you.”

“I’ll break the speed limit getting there.”

CHARLIE MEETS BOB

“Dad, what book do you have your nose buried in now?”

Charlie lowered the book to his lap and answered, “Lawrence Sanders one of his private eye stories. I enjoy his characters and writing style very much.”

“Now that I’ve interrupted you, can you indulge your daughter and divert your attention for a few minutes?”

“Of course, princess. My time is your time.”

“Thanks. My pilot friend has the weekend off and I was wondering…”

“Hold it right there, my darling daughter. You haven’t even told me this young man’s name. How about starting over?”

“Oh Dad, I’m sorry. I didn’t realize…Robert Morrisey is his name. I guess I’m a bit flustered and…”

“In love,” Charlie said softly.

Sharon hesitated a moment before agreeing, “Yes, yes. I think I am in love with him. He's the only man for me." She grasped her father's hand and sighed, "I do love Bob, I do."

"I'm happy for you, princess. I know you're mature enough to make the right choice. Now, please get us each a glass of wine. There's a bottle of champagne in the fridge. We have a very important toast to make."

"Dad, I love you." She kissed him tenderly. "I'll get the wine."

Sitting beside each other with glasses poised, Charlie toasted, "To the happiness of my dear daughter and her gentleman."

As they sipped the wine, she asked, "Could you take Bob up in the WACO Saturday or Sunday? He's never been in an open cockpit airplane."

"Sure! Sunday morning would be a good time. You know, two people fit into the front cockpit. Why don't both of you go?"

"That would be wonderful. I'll tell Bob to meet us at your hangar. How about ten o'clock?"

"Fine with me. We'll just cruise around awhile and enjoy the beautiful scenery.

Charlie had something in mind besides just looking at scenery on the flight but kept it to himself. He and Sharon got to the airport early. Charlie ran up the engine and did the preflight check. The bird was ready to fly.

Bob arrived at exactly ten o'clock, and Sharon introduced the two men.

"Pleased to meet you, Bob."

"My pleasure," Bob smiled. "Sharon has told me about some of your flying exploits."

"She probably exaggerated. How do you like flying jets?"

"I love it. The only downside is so much time away from home. But it's my career, what I want to do."

"Very good. I understand. Well, come on, let's go. I have the old leather helmets that plug into my intercom for you two. You'll be able hear me but can't talk to me. I'll see that you're buckled in and connected properly."

The WACO roared down the runway and rose gracefully into the sky. A solid ceiling of clouds at ten thousand feet assured a reasonably good day for flying. Charlie would stay below the overcast.

On the intercom Charlie advised, “We’ll cruise at five thousand feet and head south toward Colorado Springs.”

Near the springs, he asked, “Would you like to do a loop and a barrel roll? Shake heads to answer.”

His two passengers looked at each other then nodded affirmatively. Sharon’s scream at the top of the loop could not be heard over the roar of the engine. As they pulled out of the loop, Bob held up his hand and formed a circle with his thumb and forefinger. Charlie knew they would get a thrill from that maneuver. Then, without warning, he started a slow roll. When they were upside down, Charlie stopped the roll for a few seconds then continued around until they were upright again.

“Okay, folks, we’ll head west now. There’s a small airport with full facilities there called Meadow Lake where we can refuel and get a cup of coffee.” Charlie radioed Meadow Lake but didn’t expect an answer. It was such a small airfield that the radio was not always monitored. After two tries with no contact, Charlie reverted to standard safety rules, swiveling his head looking for other aircraft. None were in sight.

He descended to one thousand feet as he approached the airfield, flew directly over the grass runway to look at its condition, and turned into a landing pattern. The wind sock hung limp.

Turning to final approach, the WACO descended slowly and Charlie made a perfect three-point landing. “You two go on to the coffee shop. I’ll see to refueling.”

While the aircraft was being serviced, Charlie walked along the flight line noting that some of the hangars and taxi strips were well away from the main buildings. There was a dirt road around the edge of the entire airfield. Charlie thought, this is the place to bring our gold.

He joined Sharon and Bob for a cup of coffee before heading back to Centennial. They parked at Charlie's hangar and jumped from the lower wing to the ground.

"What a wonderful flight," Bob enthused. "The open cockpit, the low altitude, and speed make for great sightseeing. Thanks, Mr. Buckholtz."

"We'll do it again soon, and next time we'll do a four-point snap roll. Bob, nice to meet you. I've got some work to do here. Can you take Sharon home?"

"Yes, of course."

"Okay. See you both later."

DUTCH

"Joey, we're gonna meet with a guy who just might bankroll our scheme. He wants to get together with the three of us tomorrow at Luigi's bar. Know where that is?"

"Yeah."

"Meet me outside at nine o'clock. I'll call Murph now and let him know."

Joey was there when Mike arrived at Luigi's. They waited outside for Murph. Before going in, Mike briefed his fellow conspirators. "Dutch is the guy's name. We're meeting him in the back room. You guys keep your traps shut unless he asks you a question. I'll do the talking, and if he likes what he hears, we'll be on our way. He wants to size us up before he gets into the deal. Come on."

They went into the dimly lit, noisy bar and went directly to the back room. A tough looking guy blocked the door. He was all muscle and weighed about two hundred fifty pounds. His brush cut hair and clean-shaven face with a two-inch scar on the left cheek gave him an imposing look. But a pearl earring in his right ear offset that look. He was dressed entirely in black except for his socks, which matched the earring.

Mike gave their names and said, "We're here to see Dutch."

The big man studied them for a moment then motioned for them to enter the room. He stayed at the door while Mike, Joey, and Murph approached a table where a small slender man sat.

"Luna, get us a pitcher of beer and glasses, and give the bartender this C-note. Tell him to split it with Luigi."

As Luna left the room, Mike started to speak but stopped as Dutch held up both hands, palms facing Mike.

"Wait. After we get the beer. Luna doesn't have a need to know." Dutch leaned back in his chair, clasped his hands together in his lap, and closed his bleary eyes. He probably weighs all of one hundred twenty pounds, Mike thought. His eyes seemed to be constantly tearing. The only feature that seemed right on Dutch's face was the pencil thin mustache, perfectly trimmed. He was dressed in a well-tailored light gray pin stripe suit. His shoes were dark gray.

Murph, not in his usual slouch, sat ramrod-straight looking at Dutch. He imagined himself in a seat of power, just like the relaxed Dutch. Mike and Joey sat rigid and quiet. The door opened and Luna entered carrying a tray with a pitcher of beer and glasses on it.

"Wait outside the door, Luna. Nobody comes in," Dutch ordered. "Pour the beer, Mike, then introduce your friends." Mike quickly followed the order.

"Now," Dutch urged, "tell me the story."

Mike started with the overheard conversation at the Rathskeller, and then on to the tape recordings, the helicopter trip and, finally, the map.

"You got the map?" Dutch asked sharply.

" A copy, not the original," Mike replied, pulling a map from his pocket. "I marked this one just like the one in the hangar office." Mike slid the map to Dutch and pointed out the flight route and the circled X near Ohio Peak. He waited for a response.

Dutch looked at the map, rubbed his eyes, and said, "Not much detail here. Where's the rock cliff you mentioned?"

Mike pointed out a red circle he had made at the approximate location.

"How sure are you of the location of the gold?"

"It all adds up, Dutch. The clincher is the marked map in the desk drawer. Also, we have to consider what we heard about using a different airport to bring out the gold. I think we have to find the gold in the mountains before they get back to it."

Dutch sat back and rubbed his eyes again. He sat silently for a full minute, and then turned to Joey and Murph. "You guys as sure as Mike is on this deal?"

Murph quickly replied, "It's the best shot I've ever seen to grab a big bundle, Dutch."

Dutch glared at Murph. He didn't like familiarity coming from a stranger.

Joey broke the silence. "We've checked every angle. It all fits like Mike says. The gold is there."

Dutch turned to Mike. "You say the only way to get in there is by helicopter, right?"

"Yes, sir."

"Any idea how much money…Never mind. I'll find out what a chopper costs and check this out with the big man. I'll call ya, Mike, day after tomorrow." He rose from his chair, went to the door, and tapped it twice. Luna opened it instantly and they were gone.

"What d'ya think, Mike," Joey asked.

"I've got a good feeling about this. If he's taking this to the big man, that's a sign he likes it and will push for it. But remember, they'll want their cut, and I don't know how that split will come out. We'll have to wait and see. I'll let you guys know soon as I get the call. Come on. Let's go."

15

THE RICHEST GOLD ORE

A DREARY, SULLEN DAY greeted the people of Denver. A solid band of gray clouds drizzled steadily, blotting out the sky.

Jean sat at her living room picture window, staring at the gloom outside, thinking of Charlie and wishing he was here with her. The mailman plodded up the steps to her mailbox. Maybe there would be cheerful news in one of the envelopes. She was wrong.

Among the usual junk mail was a personal letter with no return address on it, but the postmark was Nassau, Bahamas. Jean didn't want to open it. She knew what Tom would write. Her suspicion was confirmed as she read his scribbling. Picking up the telephone she dialed Charlie's number.

"Good morning, Charlie. How are you on this dismal day?"

"I'm fine, Jean. You're right. It is a miserable day. You okay?"

"Oh yes, but I got a disturbing letter today from Tom."

"Oh, oh. What does that good-for-nothing say?"

"He's worried about his share of the gold and wants to know when he'll get his money. Would you answer the letter for me?"

"Sure. No problem. Now, better sit down because I have some fabulous news."

"I'm already in my recliner and ready for any good news."

"Okay. I got a preliminary report over the phone from my friend Olie. He says our ore samples are the richest they've seen in many, many years. The estimate is thirty-five to forty percent gold. How about that?"

"My goodness, sounds wonderful. Guess we hit a really rich vein. How does that translate into dollars?"

"That's hard to figure. I checked the paper today and the precious metals report lists gold at $264.00 a troy ounce. Suppose, after smelting, we got ten pounds of pure gold. That's $45,440.00 for a lump you could hold in your hand."

"Wow!"

"Jean, I have an idea. Have your chauffeur bring you over to my house and we'll celebrate. I'll make a spaghetti dinner. I have Italian bread and a bottle of Chianti wine. You bring the champagne. Bring Tom's letter too."

"Sounds great. I'll be there in about an hour. This brightens up my day as good as sunshine. Bye, bye."

"Murph, we're in business. Dutch convinced the big man that we had a good shot at the gold and they're already setting up the details the chopper, the pilot and supplies. We'll be ready to go to the mountains in about a week. I'll let you know where and when to meet."

"Man, that's great. I'm ready now."

Mike called Joey and relayed the same message.

"A toast to our fabulous gold treasure," Charlie smiled.

"To the gold and us," Jean added.

"Before we partake of my famous Italian dinner, I'd like to tell you what I have in mind for our flight to the Arrow mine. Because you're not enthusiastic about continuing our work there, I think we should just make one trip to bring out gold. Is that agreeable?"

"I really don't want to go back to that wild, treacherous place. And I don't want you and Jake to go either. It's too dangerous, and we don't have to do it. But I'll agree to one trip, only one, as long as I go with you."

"Thanks. We should be able to bring out enough to satisfy even Tom as long as the vein doesn't give out. I'll call about getting the chopper again a week from now. I'll tell Jake our plans and let you know when to plan on leaving.

"One more adventure in the mountains with no mountain lions or bears, I hope. How about a ride in the WACO before the trip?"

"Sure. Let's go the day after tomorrow. I'll show you the airport near Colorado Springs where we'll take the gold."

"And what do we do with it there?"

"I think we should have a Brinks truck waiting there to take the ore directly to the foundry for processing. I'll talk to Olie and see if he thinks that's the way to go."

"How about Sharon? Do you think she'll go with us?"

"I doubt it. She's getting serious about her new boyfriend. I think she'll want to stay here."

"Well, I guess we're all set. Let's have your famous pasta dinner and another glass of wine."

"Yes, darling. It's ready."

DUTCH'S CAPER PLAN

The meeting took place in a small park in the suburbs of Denver. They sat at a picnic table in an open-sided gazebo. The park was deserted except for two players on the tennis court. Dutch and one of his men, Louie, sat at one end of the table. Louie was a short, fat man with a cigarette dangling almost constantly from his mouth. The ashes drifted down onto his black suit, some of it now gray. His bald crown was partially covered by strands of long hair combed over from the sides and sprayed into place. He seemed to be a bundle of nerves, twitching and looking anxiously at Dutch.

Mike, Joey, and Murph sat on one side. Luna, Dutch's bodyguard, stood outside the gazebo constantly scanning the surroundings. No one would get close enough to overhear.

"All right, you guys, listen up," Dutch growled. "We've gone over all the angles of this caper. The place to land the chopper should be easy to spot. It's got to be the only clearing near a bare rock cliff, about twelve miles southwest of Ohio peak. Here's the plan. We drop you three guys off there with all the equipment and supplies you'll need, including two rifles, two pistols, and ammo. The chopper will be back for you in three days. It might take you guys a day to find the mine. It has to be near the clearing. When you find it, dig out as much gold as you can and bag it. Take the bags to the clearing for the chopper to pick up."

The chopper will be back about noon of the third day. You better be ready. Any questions?"

"What about the pilot," Mike asked. "Can he be trusted to keep his trap shut?"

"Of course. He's one of our men."

"What's the split? How much is your take?" Murph queried.

"We're paying all expenses so our cut is sixty percent. That's firm, no negotiating."

Murph, Mike, and Joey looked at each other and nodded. They knew you didn't argue with these people.

"How do we get the gold out of the ore?" Mike asked.

"Don't concern yourself with that. We've got people to handle that."

"How do we know we'll get our forty percent," Murph whined.

Dutch glared at Murph with a withering look of disdain and turned to Mike. "You better educate this bum, Mike. He don't know who he's dealin' with."

"Right, Dutch," Mike said quickly. "Keep your trap shut, Murph."

Murph's shoulders drooped and he scowled at the table.

Dutch continued, "At eight o'clock next Friday morning the helicopter will be at a farm house halfway between Foxton and Buffalo Creek. It's a two-story white house with a sign out front that says Becker's. We own it. The chopper will be behind the big red barn. Park behind the house and walk to the barn. Here's a map that shows how you get there. Okay?"

Mike looked at the map. "Yeah, we'll find it."

"All right," Dutch continued. "Another thing. We have to consider weather. Our pilot will start checking forecasts Wednesday and will let me know by Thursday evening if he has to postpone the trip. I'll call you Mike. If you don't get the call, you go. Questions?"

"Are you going with us Mr., ah, Dutch?" Joey asked.

Dutch smiled. He liked the attempt at formality. "What, an old man like me. No way, Joey. I don't like flyin'. One more thing... Wait a minute, I want to see how Luna handles those two people comin' this way."

They were all silent as they watched Luna take a few steps toward the twosome and hold up his hands. He was an imposing figure towering over the two smaller people. They listened intently to Luna near the picnic area. The tennis players left quickly.

"Good. I told him no rough stuff. Now, back to our operation. We've given you guys five days of rations, no whiskey or beer included. If weather delays your helicopter pick up, you'll have enough food and water. Don't worry, we'll get you out of there. You guys better wear jeans and bring a heavy jacket. It can get real cold at night up in the mountains. Have any one of you had experience in the wilderness?"

Mike and Murph shook their heads. Joey spoke up. "I've been hiking and camping overnight in the mountains."

Dutch nodded at Joey. "Louie, have I covered everything?"

"Just in case they're curious, boss, tell 'em what happens when they get back to the farmhouse."

"Yeah, you're right. We'll have men and transportation there to handle the gold ore. You guys are through with the caper there. I'll keep you informed, Mike, and we'll get the forty percent to you. Then you take care of Joey and Murph. Unless you guys have any more questions, that's it. Let's get out of here."

FLIGHT PLAN TO GOLD

A gentle breeze swept down from the mountains into Denver and freshened the clear, sunny afternoon. Darrae had just finished preparing for the meeting. Coffee, iced tea, soft drinks, beer, and snacks were set out near the chairs on the patio. As she stretched her long body on a chaise and sipped iced tea, her hot pink sweater was stretched to its limit by her ample bosom. Jade green slacks fit as snugly as the sweater, further accentuating her shapely figure. Sunlight caressed her ash blond hair, her dangling gold earrings, and complimented her perfect complexion. Her mind roamed into the mountain wilderness trying to picture what Jake had described. She looked forward to hearing more and was anxious to meet Jake's friends.

Jake came out to the patio. "Looks like you have everything ready. They should be here any time now."

The doorbell rang. Darrae jumped up from the chaise as Jake went to the door. He led Charlie, Jean, and Sharon to the patio and introduced them to his wife before pouring drinks for everyone.

"You certainly have a marvelous view of the mountains here," Jean observed.

"Yes," Darrae's hazel eyes sparkled. "We enjoy it so much."

Small talk went on for several minutes, then Jake interjected, "Okay, Charlie, we all know what this meeting is about, so how about updating us and filling in the details?"

"All right. But first, Darrae, I assume Jake told you about our venture in the mountains, right?"

"Yes, and he emphasized the importance of secrecy."

"Good. Our purpose now is to plan our next move in Operation Gold, as I call it. The preliminary report from the assayer rates the ore as containing thirty-five to forty percent gold. That's the richest they've seen in many years. My idea, already approved by Jean, is to make one, and only one, trip to bring out the gold ore. Because the vein is so rich I believe one trip is sufficient."

"Translate that into dollars, Charlie," Jean suggested.

"At today's price, a ten pound chunk of pure gold would be worth about forty-five thousand dollars."

"Wow!" Darrae exclaimed.

"I propose that we fly to the mine next Saturday. I've already leased the helicopter. Jake, Jean, and I will make the trip. Sharon, I presume you're too busy to go. Am I right?"

"Yes, Dad, I do have a lot of commitments. And to be perfectly honest, I don't want to ever go into that wild area with mountain lions and bears again."

"How about you, Darrae? How would you like to go with us?" Charlie asked.

"No way! I'm a city girl, and I don't want to be around wild animals except at the zoo!"

"Okay. No problem. Late next Friday afternoon, I'll get the helicopter and bring it to my hangar. Jake, before that, you and I will get everything we need into the hangar, including food and drinks. Jean, you don't have to bring anything this time."

"You're so thoughtful, Charlie. Are you going to keep lions and bears away from me too?"

"Of course, my dear. We'll lift off at ten the next morning. Of course, that's if the weather is good. I'll make a last check Friday evening. It should only take us two days, three at the most, depending on how the vein plays out. We'll bring back the chunks like we did before. Any questions, folks?"

"What about the return flight?" Jake asked. "Do we come back to Centennial or some other airfield?"

"Oh yes. I forgot to tell you my plan for that. I've decided that Centennial is too crowded. I'd like to bring the gold to a smaller, less busy airfield, Meadow Lake, just east of Colorado Springs. I've already checked it out. I'm going to ask my friend at the assay office for advice on how to get the ore safely to the foundry. My thought is that an armored truck should meet us at Meadow Lake. If Olie doesn't have a better idea, I'll make arrangement with Brinks. Anything else?"

All four people shook their heads.

Darrae replied, "Good luck, you brave adventurers. Be careful."

Jake answered, "Don't worry, honey, we won't take any chances. You can count on us to be very careful."

Charlie stood up and announced, "It's time to go to the Panorama restaurant for dinner. I've made reservations. Their specialty is all the sticky buns you can eat. But I must warn you, don't get started on them before dinner. All of their entrees are fabulous, and they're famous for their dessert cart. One more reminder. Who can tell me what it is?"

After a moment of hesitation, Jake volunteered, "I know. We can talk about anything and everything we want to at the restaurant except," he then spelled, "g-o-l-d."

"You win umpteen million dollars and a sticky bun. Come on. Let's go."

NICK' S FLIGHT TO GOLD

Following Dutch's map, on a sunny mid-August Friday, Mike easily found the Becker farmhouse. As instructed, he parked behind the house and walked with his two companions over to the big red barn. A Boeing Vertol 114 helicopter was parked there and a man climbed out of the cockpit to greet them.

"I'm Nick, your pilot. Which one of you is Mike?"

"I am," Mike answered.

"Then you other two guys must be Joey and Murph." They nodded.

"Have to be sure that I get the right guys aboard. We're all loaded with your stuff. Weather looks good so we can lift off right away. Mike, you sit up front with me. Come on. Let's go."

Nick strapped the map board to his right leg, powered up the engines, and checked the instruments. Mike noticed the route drawn on the map went through Ohio Pass just past the town of Crested Butte. They lifted off and headed southwest. The clear, blue sky calmed Murph's queasy stomach as the helicopter climbed to ten thousand feet before reaching the mountains. Joey enjoyed looking down at Buffalo Creek and Pike National Forest far below. Mike kept glancing over at Nick's map as he searched for the landmarks that would lead them to gold.

They passed over Fairplay and Nick went up to twelve thousand feet before entering Weston Pass between Mount Elbert and La Plata Peak. Just as the chopper entered the divide between the two peaks, a gust of mountain wave turbulence hit from the starboard side. The craft tilted sharply to port and plunged toward the side of La Plata. Nick fought the controls and added lift power.

In the backseat Murph grabbed an air sick bag and let go. The stench of bourbon and beer mixed with Limburger cheese permeated the cabin.

"Geez, Murph, what the hell did you do last night? Smells like you're rotten."

Murph, his face pasty white, said nothing. He couldn't. He thought he was about to die. The turbulence ceased as Nick soared through the pass, clearing the trees by three hundred feet.

Joey exclaimed, "Man, that was some flyin' Nick. I thought we'd had it. Nice goin'."

Nick only grunted. He was concentrating on keeping the chopper level. In the distance, straight ahead, he could see Crested Butte, and the air became smoother. Past Crested Butte was Ohio Peak. The air was quiet with no downdrafts and as they passed the peak Nick started a slow descent.

"Now, you guys, start looking for that bare rock cliff and the clearing. We're getting close." He descended to five thousand feet above the terrain about twelve miles beyond Ohio Peak and started a wide orbit. He slowly made the orbit tighter, but no one sighted the cliff or the clearing.

"I'm going up to seven thousand feet to get a wider field. Look sharp, guys. We'll find..."

Mike broke in saying, "Off to our left I saw something. Might be the cliff."

As Nick turned left and descended to four thousand feet, Mike kept his eyes on the spot. "There it is, the bare rock cliff."

"I see it," Nick replied. "We'll circle over it and find the clearing."

Two minutes later Joey shouted, "There's the clearing, over to the right a little."

Nick hovered over the spot, before starting his slow descent to a gentle touchdown. "Let's get your stuff unloaded fast. I want to lift off while this weather holds." All their gear and supplies were on the ground in less than half an hour and Nick rose into the clear mountain air and was gone.

"Look over there, across the clearing," Joey observed. "Looks like the carcass of a big animal. Let's pitch the tents right here."

"Yeah," Mike agreed.

After the tents were set up, one for supplies and two for the men, Mike said, "We've got lots of light left. Let's start looking for the mine. I wonder where we should look first."

"How about that rock cliff," Murph suggested. "Could be there in a cave."

"No, Murph. That's too far away from this clearing. It's got to be near here. Let's try the river."

At the river Joey pointed out the shiny pebbles in the riverbed. "Looks like gold nuggets," he said. "I seen 'em like that on one of my hikes. But that's not what we're after. We gotta find the mother lode, the place where these nuggets came from."

"You're right," Mike agreed, and that should be somewhere up river. Come on, follow me."

"Wait, Mike, let's take a look down river first. See those broken branches along the bank. That looks like a man-made trail. Let's see what's down there."

"Okay. Then we go up river."

They walked down the trail for a few minutes, Joey leading. Suddenly he stopped and peered into the forest. "Look at that small clearing, guys. What do you see?"

"Looks like a post with a sign on it," Mike answered. "Let's go have a look."

Joey read the sign aloud, "Arrow Claim August 6, 1997."

"What's it mean?" Murph questioned.

"It means Buckholtz has filed their claim for the gold mine."

"Man," Mike exclaimed, "that means we're close. Come on, let's go up river now."

"Let me lead, Mike. I've had a little experience trail blazin' and trackin'. Maybe I can spot where Buckholtz and his crew made a path to the mine."

When they saw the waterfall up ahead Joey stopped and remarked slowly, "They've been here, guys. See this matted down grass, and see the broken branches on the bushes. And look, this big branch is cut, not broken. That means people, not animals, walked here. Come on. Looks like we go to the waterfall."

About twenty feet from the waterfall, Joey stopped again and studied the banks of the river. "The trail stops at that rock wall beside the waterfall. Christ, where'd they go from there?"

16

THE GOOD MEETS THE BAD

AT THREE O'CLOCK ON FRIDAY AFTERNOON Charlie slowly eased the helicopter down for a soft landing in front of his hangar. Jake was waiting to tie-down the aircraft.

"Hi, Charlie. Nice landing. I've got some of our supplies just inside the door ready to load and the rest of our stuff is in your office. Jean dropped off her luggage earlier today. We'll be ready for an early lift off tomorrow."

"Good. I've got to make a couple of phone calls and get my maps. Then we'll load up."

Jean arrived an hour late on Saturday morning. She rushed into Charlie's office. "Sorry I'm late. I got a call from Tom. He's coming back to Denver in two weeks. He told me he was relieved to get your letter, but he sounded nervous. I don't know why."

"Don't worry about Tom. I can handle him. Come on, we're loaded and ready to go. The weather is ideal for flyin' in the mountains."

As they walked through the hangar past the WACO, Jean sighed. "I'm looking forward to a ride in this soon."

"As soon as we get back with the gold, my dear."

They lifted off into a clear blue sky with little wind to contend with, and headed southwest. Flying well south of La Plata Peak, they encountered no turbulence to mar their trip. They soon passed over Crested Butte and into the pass. The forbidding sight of Ohio Peak loomed ominously to the east.

"We're getting close now," Charlie announced. "Look for the bare cliff and the clearing." Charlie started an orbit as he descended and continued down to five thousand feet as three pairs of eyes searched the wilderness.

"I see the cliff off to our left," Jean shouted.

"And I see our landing pad just left of the nose of our chopper," Jake interrupted.

Charlie saw the clearing and headed for it, descending further. They reached the spot at five hundred feet above the terrain and Charlie put the helicopter down gently.

As the engines wound down Charlie bristled, "Damn! Someone else is here. See those tents off over there."

"My God," Jean gasped. "What do you think they're doing here?"

"I'll bet they're trying to jump our claim," Jake growled.

Charlie reached under the instrument panel for his pistol. As he slipped it into his pocket he told Jake, "Bring your pistol too, just in case."

"How could anybody find out? Who could it be?" Jake asked.

"Don't know, but we'll find out pretty soon. Whoever is here must have heard our chopper. You can be sure they're watching our every move."

Mike, Joey, and Murph were frustrated. Their search had proven fruitless. When darkness finally halted their hunt they had dinner, then wriggled into their sleeping bags, exhausted.

The next morning, after a quick breakfast, they began the search again. Joey couldn't find any more obvious paths. They went to the waterfall again. "It's got to be on the same side of the river as the clearing," Mike ventured. "Murph, you go into the woods along this rocky hillside and see if you spot anything. Joey and I'll check along the bank again. Meet back here in an hour."

Just after they gathered again at the waterfall, Joey held up his hand and exclaimed, "Listen! I hear a chopper."

"You're right," Mike agreed. "Must be our friend Buckholtz and crew. Too soon for our chopper. Come on, down to the clearing.

Murph, you get behind the tents. Joey and I'll spread out from there. No shooting yet. They'll tell us where the gold is or else."

Jean, you stay in the helicopter. Jake and I'll go out and look around."

"Oh, Charlie," Jean cried. "Let's just leave. We don't need this. It's too dangerous."

"If we have to, we'll give 'em some of the gold. Maybe we can reason with them. We can't just abandon our claim. Don't worry, we'll be careful. Come on, Jake."

Charlie and Jake jumped down and looked all around. Seeing no one they moved quickly toward the bear carcass.

"Hold it right there, you guys," a voice yelled from the forest. "We've got three guns on you. No quick moves. Stop!"

EVERYONE TO THE GOLD

Mike emerged from behind the carcass and Joey came out of the bushes nearby. Murph joined the gathering near the helicopter

"First thing you do, Buckholtz, is get the little lady out of the chopper," Mike ordered as he aimed his pistol at Charlie.

"All right, but don't get trigger happy. Jean," Charlie shouted, "come on down here." Jean climbed down from the helicopter.

"Second thing, Mr. B," Mike said, "tell us where the gold is."

"And if we don't tell you, what then?"

"You don't really want to know. My friend Murph here," Mike pointed to Murph, "gets a big charge out of making people talk. And it isn't a pretty sight. You don't want him to go to work on your lady friend, do you?" Murph grinned and giggled at the thought.

"Of course not. What would you say to our sharing the gold with you?"

"No deal. We've got three weapons trained on you. Joey, frisk the two guys and Murph pat down the lady." Murph smirked at Jean.

"Don' t you touch me, you scum," Jean hissed.

"She doesn't have a gun," Charlie bristled. "Leave her alone."

"Joey," Mike interrupted, "hold her quiet while Murph checks."

Murph moved to Jean as Joey pinned her arms behind her back. Murph's hands moved slowly up her body and paused on her breasts. He squeezed them.

Jean said nothing but spat in his face.

"You bitch, I'll…"

Charlie jumped at Murph, but Mike put his pistol on Charlie's neck saying, "Stop right there, Buckholtz. Murph, you can have fun later. Right now we go to the gold. Joey, put their guns in our tent. Then we follow these three to the gold."

Charlie and Mike led the way to the waterfall. Joey and Murph prodded Jake and Jean to follow. Jean mumbled, "bastard" as Murph poked her in the ribs. Jake added, "Dirty scum bastards."

Charlie stopped suddenly and said, "You'll need a flashlight or a lantern, mister…what's your name?"

"I don't have a name. Why a flashlight?"

"You'll see when we get there."

"Murph, go back and get our big flashlight."

They continued their trek to the waterfall. Charlie stopped as they came to the rock wall next to the falls. "See that narrow ledge," Charlie pointed. "We go along that to a cave. That's where we need a light."

"Give me the flashlight, Murph," Mike said. "Buckholtz and I'll go first. The rest of you follow."

Charlie edged slowly and carefully along the ledge, and Mike followed his footsteps exactly. Murph brought up the rear, behind Jean. Using Charlie's method of hugging the wall and taking slow sliding steps, they all got to the cave.

"Give me the flashlight, gunslinger, and I'll show you around," Charlie growled.

"Okay, but no funny stuff. Remember we have the guns."

Charlie aimed the flashlight at the rear of the cave. "That pile of rocks has been chipped out of the cave walls. There's some gold in them but not enough to be worth while." He aimed the beam of light up and slowly moved it to the wall on the right. "There's the mother lode. Look along the surface in the light. That's a rich seam of gold."

Mike grabbed the flashlight and stepped over to the wall. "Joey, Murph, come here. Look at this. The wall's loaded with gold."

"Sure is," Joey beamed.

"We're rich!" Murph gasped.

"Well, Buck," Mike sneered, "you did the smart thing showing us the gold. Now, we're all going back for some grub and get ready to work the mine tomorrow. You guys pitch your tents near ours, and we'll all get a good rest provided you guys don't try anything heroic. Get a good night's sleep. You're going to be working hard tomorrow, the lady included. And tonight, all night, one of us will be awake making sure you don't try any funny stuff."

The two factions separated and made their own cooking fires. As they ate sitting on logs around their fire, Charlie kept watching the claim jumpers. After supper as they were having coffee, Charlie whispered, "I think there's a way out of this predicament. Tomorrow watch for a time when they're all at the back of the cave. Then get up beside me at the entrance."

"Here's the reason. When we were in the cave today I noticed water dripping from the cave roof. That means the river above it is starting to break through. Think of this. For years that river flow has been slowly eroding the rock above the cave. Where it's dripping is the weak point for a break-through of the rushing river water. I figure just the right action might help it along and flood the cave."

"So what's the right action?" Jake asked.

"Wait a minute, Charlie. What happens to us? How do we escape the collapsing cave roof?" Jean questioned.

"Okay, first the right action. That cretin, Murph is unstable and I think he can be tricked into doing what we need. He's lazy and will probably be holding the gun on us most of the time while the other two work the vein. I'll start with some mild insults, then question his ability as a marksman, and goad him into firing a shot into the crack in the cave roof. The impact of the bullet plus the sound wave in the confines of the cave could trigger the roof collapse."

"Now, how do we escape? The three of us are together at the

mouth of the cave. As soon as the roof starts coming down we turn and jump into the falling water. We should go into the deep pool at the bottom of the falls and be okay. Those thieves will be buried under tons of rock and rushing water."

"And if it doesn't work, the roof doesn't collapse, what then?" Jake posed.

"We'll just have to devise an alternate plan."

Jean whispered softly, "Charlie, I can't swim. I'll drown."

"No, my dear, the force of the water will push you under and down the river in only a few seconds. Just hold your breath and I'll be there to grab you and get you out of the water."

"Sure sounds risky, but I suppose we have to try it."

"Yes, we do. Those guys aren't going to let us out of here alive after they get the gold."

CLOUDS OF DOOM

Distant rumbles of thunder and a granite gray sky announced the beginning of the next day. Gusts of cold wind chased ominous clouds across the sky as they seethed and boiled into anvil shapes. The beginning of day promised miserable weather and had the sense of impending doom.

"Hurry up, you three laborers," Mike shouted. "We're going to the cave in fifteen minutes. You're going to help dig and load ore and carry our gear and bags."

Charlie sauntered over to their tormentors. "Hope you're going to do some heavy work too. How about leaving Jean here to fix lunch for us?"

"No way. She goes with us so Murph can keep an eye on her."

"I doubt Murph can shoot straight if he's keeping his eyes on her."

"Just try me, big man, just try," Murph growled.

"Come on, grab the tools. Joey, get the cooler and Murph, you go last with a gun on 'em," Mike ordered.

At the waterfall, Charlie said, "Looks like it's going to rain like hell while we're in the cave. At least we can stay dry in there."

Mike led the way along the wet ledge. Joey slipped and would have fallen into the waterfall, but Jake grabbed him and held him on the ledge. Joey said nothing but smiled at Jake. It was his unsaid thank you.

Inside the cave Charlie pointed out that only two people could chip ore at the same time. He took a pickaxe and instructed, "You need to chip out pieces about one inch deep that weigh one to two pounds. That's the way the U.S. Bureau of Mines assay people want it. Let me show you." He cut into the vein and pried out a chunk. "That's about the size they want to process at the foundry."

"Okay," Mike said, "you and I will start. Murph, you check that pile of rocks at the back of the cave. See if any of them show a lot of gold. Jake, you help him. Joey, see if you can find a ledge to put the lantern on then sit near the mouth of the cave with the gun. Lady, take this flashlight and stay with Joey. We might need more light."

After an hour of work at the cave wall, Mike and Charlie put their chunks of ore in canvas bags. Mike checked to see if Murph found any worthwhile rocks. He hadn't.

Joey and Jake were next to attack the vein of gold. Charlie got cans of soda from the cooler for Mike, Murph, Jean, and himself and joined Jean at the mouth of the cave. Mike went to the back of the cave with Murph.

A loud clap of thunder startled everyone. Charlie declared, "We've got a whopping big thunderstorm out there. Good thing we're in here. You won't have to shoot us, Murph. We're not going to escape into that storm. Although your aim is probably so bad you'd miss us both and hit Joey."

"I'm just waitin' for you to make a break for it, hero," Murph smirked. "You'd find out real quick how good my aim is."

Jake put down his pickaxe and said, "I need a cold drink. I'll be right back, Joey." Jake went to the cooler, got a coke, and stood next to Jean.

"Tell you what, Murph. See that crack in the cave roof where the water's dripping. You put a bullet in there and I'll believe you can hit what you aim at."

Murph looked up. “Man, that’s a cinch. I’ll plug that drip with a bullet.”

Mike quickly interjected, “You better get it right in the crack. We don’t need a ricocheting bullet in here.”

“Fifty bucks says you can’t do it,” Charlie challenged.

“You’re on, hero. Mike, shine your flashlight up there.” Murph raised his pistol, steadied his right arm with his left, and gently squeezed the trigger.

The noise was thunderous and nearly deafening as it echoed in their ears. A split second later there was blinding flash of lightning at the mouth of the cave. The roof of the cave started to crumble.

Charlie, Jean, and Jake turned in unison and jumped into the cascade. They couldn’t hear the screams of terror in the cave. Falling rock and rushing water silenced all human sound as the cave collapsed.

As Jake plunged into the pool at the bottom of the waterfall, a falling rock from the cave struck his right shoulder. He knew he was hurt and struggled to get downstream. Jean was pushed deep into the pool. Holding her breath, she fought her way up. Charlie surfaced and stroked frantically over to Jean. He grabbed her and swam with the current until his feet touched the riverbed.

Jake struggled to swim with one arm. Charlie got Jean to the riverbank and seeing that Jake was in trouble dove in and was quickly at his side. Blood was flowing from Jake’s right shoulder. Charlie put an arm around Jake’s chest and pulled toward the bank.

“Jean, run get our first aid kit. Jake’s hurt.” Charlie helped Jake lie down, ripped off his shirt, and pressed it to Jake’s shoulder.

A sodden, dripping Jean knelt beside Jake with the first aid kit. “Let me see, Charlie. Oh dear. We’ve got to clean it and stop the bleeding. I don’t think the wound is deep enough to have injured any bones.” After disinfecting the wound, she wrapped the shoulder in gauze. A sling fashioned from one of her blouses held the shoulder motionless. As they walked back to the clearing, the clouds disappeared and the rain stopped.

Back at camp, Charlie brewed coffee and helped Jake into dry clothes. Jake rested on a bedroll in the tent. Jean came out of her tent in dry jeans and one of Charlie's shirts. She had even fixed her hair.

"You look as beautiful as ever, Jean. But in your soaked clothes you would have easily won any wet t-shirt contest."

"Don't you try to sweet talk me, Mr. Buckholtz. You've got to get us out of here fast and get Jake to a doctor. This is it, my darling. This is the end of operation Arrow."

"I know, you're right. We'll leave first thing in the morning. We can't go now, not enough daylight left to fly the mountains."

"All right. Let's start packing."

Within a short time they were ready to leave except for taking down the tents. After a light supper Charlie said, "Jake, you okay to stay here while Jean and I take a last look at the waterfall?"

"Yeah, I'm okay. You two go ahead."

Charlie and Jean stared silently at the altered scene. A sloping tumble of boulders replaced the cave. The waterfall was reduced in size and volume. They stood beside the pool as the ever-rushing river continued its journey. Charlie bent down and picked up a small rock. "Look, Jean, one of the ore samples. Look at that bright, shiny gold."

"The last we'll see of the Arrow mine."

"Absolutely," Charlie commented as he shoved the chunk in his pocket.

Early the next morning they lifted off and flew northeast.

They didn't look back. As they passed over Fairplay, Charlie muttered, "Look to our left, about ten o'clock. There's a chopper headed southwest. Wonder if it's..."

"We don't want to know," Jean interrupted. "Let's just look forward to this, our final flight."

EPILOGUE

Charlie and Jean were married in a small chapel with only relatives and close friends as guests. Their honeymoon was a flight in the WACO to several scenic places around the country.

Jean sold all of her properties, stocks and bonds, and even her house. She gave five million dollars to her son, and millions to several charities including the Battle of Normandy Museum in France.

Charlie and Jean bought a small chalet near Manitou Springs on a hillside at the entrance to Ute Pass. The chunk of gold ore Charlie found was placed on the fireplace mantel.

Sharon married Bob and nine months later gave birth to twins.

Jake and Darrae were given a bonus of five hundred thousand dollars by Jean.

Tom returned to Denver with the HIV virus. He had contracted the deadly disease in Nassau. Jean gave him one hundred thousand dollars.

Nick, the helicopter pilot, waited for his passengers for twenty-four hours, gave up, and returned to Denver. He reported to Dutch that Mike, Joey, and Murph were missing.

Jean learned to fly the WACO. Charlie said she was a "natural."

Printed in the United States
25188LVS00001B/418